I0595288

Mary Elizabeth Braddon

All along the River
A Novel. Vol. 2

ISBN/EAN: 9783337046576

Printed in Europe, USA, Canada, Australia, Japan

Cover: Foto ©Andreas Hilbeck / pixelio.de

More available books at **www.hansebooks.com**

ALL ALONG THE RIVER

A Novel

BY THE AUTHOR OF

"ISHMAEL," "VIXEN," "LADY AUDLEY'S SECRET,"
ETC., ETC.

IN THREE VOLUMES
VOL. II.

LONDON
SIMPKIN, MARSHALL, HAMILTON, KENT & CO.
LIMITED
STATIONERS' HALL COURT
1893

LONDON:
PRINTED BY WILLIAM CLOWES AND SONS, LIMITED,
STAMFORD STREET AND CHARING CROSS.

Mary Elizabeth Braddon

All along the River

A Novel. Vol. 2

CONTENTS OF VOL. II.

ALL ALONG THE RIVER.

CHAPTER I.

"SAY THE FALSE CHARGE WAS TRUE."

THE Baynhams' dinner-party was a function to be anticipated with horror, and undergone with resignation. For the first week after the acceptance of the invitation the ceremony had seemed so far off that it could be talked about lightly, and even made an occasion for mirth—Allegra giving her own little sketch of what a dinner at Myrtle Lodge would be like—the drawing-room with its wealth of chair-backs and photograph albums, and the water-colour landscapes which Mrs. Baynham had painted while she was at a finishing school at Plymouth, never having touching brush or pencil since—and Mrs. Baynham's rosy-cheeked nieces from Truro, who always appeared on the scene of any festivity. Yes, one could tell beforehand what the entertainment would be like.

One thing they did not know, however, Mrs. Baynham having been discreetly silent on the subject. They did not know that they were to meet the Glenaveril family in full force, the doctor's wife being of opinion that a friendly dinner-party was the panacea for all parish quarrels and small antagonisms, and that by judiciously bringing the Crowthers and the Disneys together at a well-spread board, and in the genial atmosphere of her unspacious drawing-room, she could bring about an end of the feud, or tacit coldness, which had divided the Angler's Nest and Glenaveril since Colonel Disney's home-coming. It was a disappointment to this worthy woman to see Vansittart Crowther, when Colonel and Mrs. Disney were announced, start and glare as if a mad dog had been brought into the room; but she was relieved at seeing the easy nod which the colonel bestowed upon his vanquished foe, and the friendly hand which good Mrs. Crowther held out to Isola, who paled and blushed, and all but wept at meeting with that cordial matron.

"I don't know why you never come to see me," said Mrs. Crowther, confidentially, having made room for Isola upon a very pretentious and uncomfortable sofa of the cabriole period, a sofa with a sloping seat and a stately back in three oval divisions, heavily framed in carved walnut, a back against which it was an agony to lean, a seat upon which it was a struggle to sit. "But I don't see why we shouldn't be friends when we do happen to meet."

"Dear Mrs. Crowther, we are always friends. I shall never forget your kindness to me."

"There, there; you're a tender-hearted soul, I know. It grieved me so not to go and see you when you were ill; and not to pay attention to your baby. Such a sweet little fellow, too. I've given him many a kiss on the sly when I've met him and his nurse in the lanes. I suppose Mr. Crowther and the colonel don't hit their horses very well together. That's at the bottom of it all, no doubt. But as for you and me, Isola, I hope we shall always be good friends."

This confidential talk between the two women,

observed by Mrs. Baynham out of the corner of her eye, augured well; but Mr. Crowther had not left off glaring, and a glare in those protruding eyeballs was awful. He usurped the hearthrug, as he laid down the law about the political situation and the impending ruin of the country.

"A feeble policy never maintained the prestige of any country, sir," he told Captain Pentreath, the half-pay bachelor, who was devoted to fishing, and cared very little whether his country had prestige or shuffled on without it—so long as fish would bite. "We lost our prestige when we lost Beaconsfield, and with our prestige we are losing our influence. The Continental powers leave us out of their calculations. The neutral policy of the last ten years has stultified the triumph of British arms from Marlborough to Wellington. The day will come, sir, when the world will cease to believe in the history of those magnificent campaigns. People will say, ' These are idle traditions. England could never have been a warlike nation.' "

Captain Pentreath tried to look interested, but was obviously indifferent to the opinion of future ages, and intent upon watching Allegra, looking her handsomest in a yellow silk gown, and deep in talk with Captain Hulbert, who leant his tall form against Mrs. Baynham's cottage piano, which, with a view to artistic effect, had been draped with striped Indian stuffs and wheeled into a position that made the room more difficult of navigation.

One only of the rosy-cheeked nieces was allowed to appear at the dinner-table; firstly because the table was a tight fit for twelve, and secondly because a thirteenth would have excited superstitious fears. The younger sister, whom people asked about with tender solicitude, was to be on view afterwards, when she would take the bass to her sister's treble in the famous overture to Zampa, which, although not exactly a novelty, may be relied upon to open a musical evening with *éclat*.

Every one had arrived, and after a chilling delay, Potts, the local fishmonger, who had been a butler, and who went out to wait at dinner-parties, and was as familiar a figure as a saddle of mutton or a cod's head and shoulders, made his solemn announcement, and with an anxious mind, Mrs. Baynham saw her guests parade across the narrow hall, somewhat overfurnished with stags' heads, barometers, gig-whips and umbrella-stands, to the dining-room, while a hot blast of roast meat and game burst fiercely from the adjacent kitchen.

Mrs. Baynham had allotted Isola to Mr. Crowther, determined to carry out her idea of bringing about a friendly feeling. Mr. Baynham took Mrs. Crowther, and Captain Pentreath had the privilege of escorting Belinda, whose sentiments and airs and graces of every kind he knew by heart. There was no more excitement in such companionship than in going in to dinner with his grandmother. What is the use of being brought in continual association with a handsome heiress if you know yourself a detrimental?

"She would no more look at me as a lover than she would at a Pariah dog," said the captain, when some officious boon companion at the club suggested that he should enter himself for the Crowther Stakes.

Captain Hulbert was made happy with Allegra, and Colonel Disney was honoured by his hostess, to whom strict etiquette would have prescribed the peer's son. There was surplus female population in the persons of Alicia Crowther and Mary Baynham, who agreeably adorned each side of the table with a little extra sweetness and light; Miss Baynham, buxom and rosy in a white cashmere frock which she had grown out of since her last dinner-party; Miss Crowther, square shouldered and bony, in a black confection by Worth, with a bloated diamond heart making a mirage upon a desert waste of chest, it being a point of honour with thin girls to be more *décoletée* than their plumper sisters.

Mrs. Baynham's conversation at one of her own dinners was apt to be somewhat distracted and inconsecutive in substance, although she maintained a smiling and delighted air all the time, whatever anxieties might be wearing her spirit—anxieties about the cooking and the attendance—angry wonder at the prolonged absence of the parlour-maid—distress at seeing the lobster sauce dragging its slow length along when people had nearly finished the turbot— agonizing fears lest the *vol au vent* should not last out after that enormous help taken by Captain Pentreath, in sheer absence of mind, perhaps, since he only messed it about on his plate, while he bored Miss Crowther with a prosy account of his latest victory over an obstinate demon of the Jack family—" such a devil of a fellow, three feet long, and with jaws like a crocodile."

Colonel Disney was almost as inconsecutive and fragmentary in his conversation as his hostess, and did not imitate her smiling aspect. He was silent and moody, as he had been at the Glenaveril dinner, more than a year ago. That Silenus face bending towards his wife's ear— that confidential air assumed in every look and tone—made him furious. He could scarcely sit through the dinner. He wounded Mrs. Baynham in her pride of heart as a housekeeper by hardly touching her choicest dishes.

" Oh, come now, Colonel Disney," she pleaded, " you must take one of my lobster cromskys. I don't mind owning that I made them myself. It is an *entrée* I learnt from the cook at my own home. My father was always particular about his table, and we had a professed cook. Please don't refuse a cromsky."

Colonel Disney took the thing on his plate, and

sat frowning at it, while a bustle at the door and a marked rise in the temperature indicated the entrance of the *pièce de resistance*, in the shape of a well-kept saddle of mutton.

"Oh, but you had seen the *Vendetta* before, hadn't you?" asked the oily voice on the other side of the table. "You knew all about her. Really, now, Mrs. Disney, was that your first visit to Lostwithiel's yacht?"

Isola looked at the speaker as if he had struck her. Great God, how pale she was! Or was it the reflection of the apple-green shade upon the candle in front of her which gave her that ghastly look?

"Yes," she said. "I saw the yacht from the harbour years ago."

"But you were never on board her? How odd, now. I had a notion that you must have seen that pretty cabin, and all Lostwithiel's finical arrangements. He was so proud of the *Vendetta* when he was here. He was always asking my girls on board. You remember, Alicia, how Lord Lostwithiel used to ask you two girls to tea?"

"Yes," answered his daughter, in her hard

voice. "He asked us often enough, but mother would not let us go."

"How very severe!" said Captain Hulbert, attracted by the sound of his brother's name. "Why do you object to a tea-party on the *Vendetta*, Mrs. Crowther? Have you a prejudice against yachts? Do you think they are likely to go down in harbour, like the poor old *Royal George?*"

"Oh no, I am not afraid of that. Only I liked Lord Lostwithiel to come to tea with us at Glenaveril; and I did not think it would be quite the thing for my girls to visit a bachelor's yacht, even if I went with them. People at Trelasco are only too ready to make unpleasant remarks. They would have said we were running after Lord Lostwithiel."

"Oh, but it isn't the single girls who run after the men nowadays," said Mr. Crowther, with his Silenus grin; "it's the young married women. They are the sirens."

Nobody took any notice of this remark; and the conversation which had become general for a minute or two resumed its duologue form.

Captain Hulbert and Allegra went on with

their animated discussion as to the author of
" Macbeth " and " Hamlet ; " and Captain Pentreath took up the thread of his story about the
obstinate pike; Alicia talked to the doctor about
her last day with the harriers; and Mary Baynham told Mrs. Crowther about a church bazaar,
which had electrified Truro, and at which she had
" helped " at somebody else's stall.

" It was hard work standing about and trying
to sell things all day, and persuading stingy old
gentlemen to put into raffles for talking dolls,"
said Miss Baynham. " I have pitied the shop-
girls ever since."

Mrs. Baynham gave the signal for departure,
feeling that her dinner, from a material point of
view, had been a success. The lobster sauce had
been backward, and the three last people to
whom the *vol au vent* was offered had got very
little except pie-crust and white sauce, but those
were small blemishes. The mutton and the
pheasants had been unimpeachable; and on those
substantial elements Mrs. Baynham took her
stand. She had spared neither pains nor money.
Her Italian cream was cream, and not corn-flour.
Her cabinet-pudding was a work of art. She

felt satisfied with herself, and knew that the doctor would approve; and yet she felt somehow that the moral atmosphere had not been altogether free from storm-cloud. Colonel Disney had looked on at the feast with a gloomy countenance; Mr. Crowther had talked in an unpleasant tone.

"I am afraid those two will never forget the church-path," she thought, as she set her nieces down to Zampa, and then went to inspect the card-table in a snug corner near the fire, with its freshly lighted wax candles, and new cards placed ready for the good old English game which our ancestors called whist.

Zampa once started meant a noisy evening. Captain Pentreath would sing "The Maid of Llangollen," and "Drink, puppy, drink." Mary Baynham would murder "It was a dream," and scream the higher notes in "Ruby." Duet would follow solo, and fantasia succeed ballad. Mrs. Baynham's idea of a social gathering being the nearest attainable approach to a penny reading. She would have had recitations, and imitations of popular actors, had there been any one capable of providing that form of amusement.

This evening, however, she failed in getting a quartette for whist. Neither Mr. Crowther nor his wife was disposed for cards; Colonel Disney coldly declined; and it was useless to ask the young people to leave the attractions of that woody piano. While she was lamenting this state of things, the whist-table being usually a feature in her drawing-room, the Disneys and Allegra bade her good night, and were gone before she had time to remonstrate with them for so early a departure.

It seemed earlier than it really was, for the dinner had been late. Disney's quick ear had heard the step of his favourite horse, punctual as the church clock. He had ordered his carriage at half-past ten, and at half-past ten he and his party left the drawing-room, the doctor following to hand the ladies to their carriage, while the colonel lighted a cigar on the door-step, preparatory to walking home.

"It's a fine night; I'd rather walk," he said.

He walked further than the Angler's Nest. He walked up to the hill where he and Isola had sat in the summer sunshine on the day after his home-coming. He roamed about that wild height for two hours, and the church clock struck one while he was in the lane leading down to Trelasco.

"If that man has any motive for his insolence —if there is any secret between him and my wife, I'll wring the truth out of him before he is a day older," the colonel said to himself, as he tramped homewards.

He wrote to Mr. Crowther next morning, requesting the favour of half an hour's private conversation upon a very serious matter. He proposed to call upon Mr. Crowther at twelve o'clock, if that hour would be convenient. The bearer of the note would wait for an answer.

Mr. Crowther replied that he would be happy to see Colonel Disney at the hour named.

The colonel arrived at Glenaveril with military punctuality, and was forthwith shown into that grandiose apartment, where all those time-honoured works which the respectable family bookseller considers needful to the culture of the country gentleman were arranged in old oak bookcases, newly carved out of soft chestnut wood in the workshops of Venice. It was an imposing apartment, with panelled dado, gilded Japanese paper, heavy cornice and ceiling, in *carton pierre*—such a room as makes the joy of architect, builder, and furniture-maker. So far as dignity and social position can be bought for money, those attributes had been bought by Vansittart Crowther; and yet this morning, standing before his mediæval fire place, with his hands in the pockets of his velvet lounge coat, he looked a craven. He advanced a step or two to meet his visitor, and offered his hand, which the colonel overlooked, fixing him at once with a gaze that went straight to the heart of his mystery. He felt that an accuser was before him—that he, Vansittart Crowther, was called to account.

"Mr. Crowther, I have come to ask what you mean by your insolent manner to my wife?"

"Insolent! My dear Colonel Disney, I admire the lady in question more than any other woman within twenty miles. Surely it is not insolent to admire a pretty woman?"

"It is insolent to adopt the tone you have adopted to Mrs. Disney—first in your own house —on the solitary occasion when my wife and I were your guests—and next at the dinner-table last night. I took no notice of your manner on the first occasion—for though I considered your conduct offensive, I thought it might be your ordinary manner to a pretty woman, and I considered I did enough in forbidding my wife ever to re-enter your house. But last night the offence was repeated—was grosser—and more distinctly marked. What do you mean by talking to my wife of Lord Lostwithiel with a peculiar emphasis? What do you mean by your affectation of a secret understanding with my wife whenever you pronounce Lord Lostwithiel's name?"

"I am not aware that there has been anything peculiar in my pronunciation of that name—or in my manner to Mrs. Disney," said Mr. Crowther, looking at his boots, but with a malignant smile lurking at the corners of his heavy lips.

"Oh, but you are aware of both facts. You meant to be insolent, and meant other people to notice your insolence. It was your way of being even with me for defying you to shut up the wood yonder, aud cut off the people's favourite walk to church. You dared not attack me; but you thought you could wreak your petty spite upon my wife—and you thought I should be too dull to observe, or too much of a poltroon to resent your impertinence. That's what you thought, Mr. Crowther: and I am here to undeceive you, and to tell you that you are a coward and a liar, and that if you don't like those words you may send any friend you please to my friend, Captain Hulbert, to arrange a meeting in the nearest and most convenient place on the other side of the channel."

Mr. Crowther turned very red, and then very pale. It was the first time he had been invited to venture his life in defence of his honour; and for the moment it seemed to him that honour was a small thing, a shadowy possession exaggerated into importance by the out-at-elbows and penniless among mankind, who had nothing else to boast of. As if a man who always kept fifty thousand pounds at his bankers, and who had money invested all over the world, would go and risk his life upon the sands of Blankenburgh against a soldier whose retiring allowance was something less than three hundred a year, and who was perhaps a dead shot. The idea was preposterous!

No, Mr. Crowther was not going to fight, and though he quailed before those steady eyes of Martin Disney's, calm in their deep indignation, this explanation was not unwelcome to him. He had a dagger ready to plunge into his enemy's heart, and he did not mean to hold his hand.

"I'm not a fighting man, Colonel Disney," he said; "and if I were I should hardly care to fight for a grass widow who made herself common talk by her flirtation with a man of most notorious antecedents. We will say that it never was any more than a flirtation—in spite of Mrs. Disney's mysterious disappearance after the Hunt Ball, which happened exactly to correspond with Lord Lostwithiel's sudden departure. The two events might have no connection—more especially as Mrs. Disney came back ten days after, and Lord Lostwithiel hasn't come back yet."

"I can answer for my wife's conduct, sir, under all circumstances, and amidst all surroundings. You are the first person who has ever dared to cast a slur upon her, and it shall not be my fault if you are not the last. I tell you again, to your face, that you are a coward and a liar—a coward because you are insolent to a young and lovely woman, and a liar because you insinuate evil against her which you are not able to substantiate."

"Ask your wife where she was at the end of December, the year before last—the year you were in India. Ask her what she had been doing in London when she came back to Fowey on the last day of the year, and travelled in the same train with my lawyer, Mr. MacAllister, who was struck by her appearance, first because she was so pretty, and next because she looked the picture of misery—got into conversation with her, and found out who she was. If you think that is a lie you can go to MacAllister, in the Old Jewry, and ask him to convince you that it is a fact."

"There is no occasion. My wife has no secrets from me."

"I am glad to hear it. Then there is really nothing to fight about except a good deal of vulgar abuse on your part, which I am willing to overlook. A man of your mature age, married to a beautiful girl, has some excuse for being jealous."

"More excuse, perhaps, than a man of your

age has for acting like a cad," said the colonel, turning upon his heel, and leaving Mr. Crowther to his reflections.

Those reflections were not altogether bitter. Mr. Crowther felt assured that he had sown the seeds of future misery. He did not believe in the colonel's assertion that there were no secrets between him and his wife. He had cherished the knowledge of that mysterious journey from London on the last day of the year. He had warned his confidential friend and solicitor to mention the fact to no one else. He had pried and questioned, and by various crooked ways had fought out that Isola had been absent from the Angler's Nest for some days after the Hunt Ball, and he had told himself that she was a false wife, and that Martin Disney was a fool to trust her.

As for being called by harsh names, he was too much a man of the world to attach any importance to an angry husband's abuse. It made him not a sixpence the poorer; and as there had been no witness to the interview it scarcely diminished his dignity. The thing rested between him and his enemy.

"He took down my gates, but I think I have given him something to think about that will spoil his rest for many a night, before he has thought it out," mused Mr. Crowther.

It was after the usual luncheon hour before Martin Disney went back to the Angler's Nest. He had been for a long walk by the river, trying to walk down the devil that raged within him, before he could trust himself to go home. His wife was alone in the drawing-room, sitting by the fire with her baby in her lap; but this time he did not pause on the threshold to contemplate that domestic picture. There was no tenderness in the eyes which looked at his wife—only a stern determination. Every feature in the familiar face looked strange and rigid, as in the face of an accuser and judge.

"Send the child away, Isola. I want some serious talk with you."

She stretched out a faltering hand to the bell, looking at him, pale and scared, but saying no word. She gave the baby to his nurse presently in the same pallid dumbness, never taking her eyes from her husband's face.

"Martin," she gasped at last, frozen by his angry gaze, "is there anything wrong?"

"Yes, there is something horribly wrong—something that means destruction. What were you doing in London the winter before last, while I was away? What was the motive of your secret departure—your stealthy return? What were you doing on the last day of the year? Where had you been? With whom?"

She looked at him breathless with horror; whether at the accusation implied in his words, or at his withering manner, it would have been difficult for the looker-on to decide. His manner was terrible enough to have scared any woman, as he stood before her, waiting for her answer.

"Where had you been—with whom?" he repeated, while her lips moved mutely, quivering as in abject fear. "Great God! why can't you answer? Why do you look such a miserable, degraded creature—self-convicted—not able to speak one word in your own defence?"

"On the last day of the year?" she faltered, with those tremulous lips.

"On the last day of the year before last—the winter I spent in Burmah. What were you

doing—where were you—where had you been?
Is it so difficult to remember?"

"No, no; of course not," she cried, with a
half-hysterical laugh. "You frighten me out of
my senses, Martin. I don't know what you are
aiming at. I was coming home from London on
that day—of course—the 31st of Jan—no, December. Coming home from Hans Place, where I
had been spending a few days with Gwendoline."

"You never told me of that visit to Gwendoline."

"Oh yes; I'm sure I told you all about it
in one of my letters. Perhaps you did not get
that letter—I remember you never noticed it in
yours. Martin, for God's sake, don't look at
me like that!"

"I am looking at you to see if you are the
woman I have loved and believed in, or if you
are as false as hell," he said, with his strong
hand grasping her shoulder, her face turned to
his, so that those frightened eyes of hers could
not escape his scrutiny.

"Who has put this nonsense in your head?"

"Your neighbour—your good Mrs. Crowther's
husband—told me that his lawyer travelled with

you from Paddington—on the 31st of December —the year before last. He got into conversation with you—you remember, perhaps?"

"No," she cried, with a sudden piteous change in her face, "I can't remember."

"But you came from London on that day. You remember that?"

"Yes, yes. I came from Gwendoline's house on that day. I told you so in my letter."

"That letter which I never received—telling me of that visit to which you made no allusion in any of your later letters. It was about that time, I think, that you fell off as a correspondent —left off telling me all the little details of your life—which in your earlier letters seemed to shorten the distance between us."

She was silent, listening to his reproaches with a sullen dumbness, as it seemed to him, while he stood there in his agony of doubt—in his despairing love. He turned from her with a heartbroken sigh, and slowly left the room, going away he scarce knew whither, only to put himself beyond the possibility of saying hard things to her, of letting burning, branding words flash out of the devouring fire in his heart.

She stood for a few moments after he had gone, hesitating, breathless, and frightened, like a hunted animal at bay—then ran to the door, opened it softly, and listened. She could hear him pacing the room above. Again she stood still and hesitated, her lips tightly set, her hands clenched, her brow bent in painful thought. Then she snatched hat and jacket from a corner of the hall where such things were kept, and put them on hurriedly, with trembling hands, as if her fate depended upon the speed with which she got herself ready to go out, looking up at the great, dim, brazen face of the eight-day clock all the while. And then she let herself out at a half-glass door into the garden, and walked quickly to a side gate that opened in to the lane—the gate at which the baker and the butcher stopped to gossip with the maids on fine mornings.

There was a cold bracing wind, and the sun was declining in a sky barred with dense black clouds—an ominous sky, prophetic of storm or rain. Isola walked up the hill towards Tyward-reath as if she were going on an errand of deadliest moment, skirted and passed the village,

with no slackening of her pace, and so by hill
and valley to Par, a long and weary walk under
ordinary circumstances for a delicate young
woman, although accustomed to long country
walks. But Isola went upon her lonely journey
with a feverish determination which seemed to
make her unconscious of distance. Her steps
never faltered upon the hard, dusty road. The
autumn wind that swept the dead leaves round
her feet seemed to hold her up and carry her
along without effort upon her part. Past copse
and meadow, common land and stubble, she
walked steadily onward, looking neither to right
nor left of her path, only straight forward to the
signal lights that showed fiery red in the grey
dusk at Par junction. She watched the lights
growing larger and more distinct as she neared
the end of her journey. She saw the fainter
lights of the village scattered thinly beyond the
station lamps, low down towards the sandy shore.
She heard the distant rush of a train, and the
dull sob of the sea creeping up along the level
shore, between the great cliffs that screened the
bay. A clock struck six as she waited at the
level crossing, in an agony of impatience, while

truck after truck of china clay crept slowly by, in a procession which seemed endless; and then for the first time she felt that the wind was cold, and that her thin little jacket did not protect her from that biting blast. Finally the line was clear, and she was able to cross and make her way to the village post-office.

Her business at the post-office occupied about a quarter of an hour, and when she came out into the village street the sky had darkened, and there were heavy rain-drops making black spots upon the grey dust of the road; but she hurried back by the way she had come, recrossed the line and set out on the long journey home. The shower did not last long, but it was not the only one she encountered on her way back, and the poor little jacket was wet through when she re-entered by the servant's gate, and by the half-glass door, creeping stealthily into her own house and running upstairs to her own room to get rid of her wet garments before any one could surprise her with questions and sympathy. It was past eight o'clock, though she had walked so fast all the way as to feel neither cold nor damp. She took off her wet clothes and dressed herself for dinner in fear and trembling, imagining that her absence would have been wondered at, and her errand would be questioned. It was an infinite relief when she went down to the drawing-room to find only Allegra sitting at her easel, working at a sepia sketch by lamplight.

"Martin is very late," she said, looking up as Isola entered, "and he is generally a model of punctuality. I hope there is nothing wrong. Where have you been hiding yourself since lunch, Isa? Have you been lying down?"

"Yes, part of the time"—hesitatingly. "It is very late."

"Twenty minutes to nine. Dale has been in twice in the last quarter of an hour to say that the dinner is being spoilt. Hark! There's the door, and Martin's step. Thank God, there is nothing wrong!" cried Allegra, getting up and going out to meet her brother.

Colonel Disney's countenance as he stood in the lamplight was not so reassuring as the substantial fact of his return. It was something to know that he was not dead, or hurt in any desperate way—victim of any of those various accidents which the morbid mind of woman can imagine if husband or kinsman be unusually late for dinner; but that things were all right with him was open to question. He was ghastly pale, and had a troubled, half-distracted expression which scared Allegra almost as much as his prolonged absence had done.

"I am sure there is something wrong!" she said, when they were seated at dinner, and the parlour-maid had withdrawn for a minute or two in pursuance of her duties, having started them fairly with the fish.

"Oh no, there is nothing particularly amiss; I have been worried a little, that's all. I am very sorry to be so unconscionably late for dinner, and to sit down in this unkempt condition. But I loitered at the club looking at the London papers. I shall have to go to London to-morrow, Isola— on business—and I want you to go with me. Have you any objection?"

She started at the word London, and looked at him curiously—surprised, yet resolute—as if she were not altogether unprepared for some startling proposition on his part.

"Of course not. I would rather go with you if you really have occasion to go."

"I really have; it is very important. You won't mind our deserting you for two or three days, will you, Allegra?" asked Disney, turning to his sister. "Mrs. Baynham will be at your service as chaperon if you want to go out anywhere while we are away. It is an office in which she delights."

"I won't trouble her. I shall stay at home, and paint all the time. I have a good deal of work to do to my pictures before they will be ready for the winter exhibition, and the time for sending in is drawing dreadfully near. You need have no anxiety as to my gadding about, Martin. You will find me shut up in my painting-room, come home when you will."

Later, when she and her brother were alone in the drawing-room, she went up to him softly and put her arms around his neck.

"Martin, dearest, I know you have some great trouble. Why don't you tell me? Is it anything very bad? Does it mean loss of fortune; poverty to be faced; this pretty home to be given up, perhaps?"

"No, no, no, my dear. The home is safe enough; the house will stand firm as long as you and I live. I am not a shilling poorer than I was yesterday. There is nothing the matter— nothing worth speaking about; blue devils, vapours if you like. That's all."

"You are ill, Martin. You have found out that there is something wrong with you—heart, lungs, something—and you are going to London to consult a physician. Oh, my dear, dear brother," she cried, with a look of agony, her arms still clasped about his neck, "don't keep me in the dark; let me know the worst."

"There is no worst, Allegra. I am out of sorts, that's all. I am going to town to see my lawyer."

CHAPTER II.

"MY LIFE CONTINUES YOURS, AND YOUR LIFE MINE."

THEY started by the eleven-o'clock train from Fowey next morning, husband and wife, in a strangely silent companionship—Isola very pale and still as she sat in a corner of the railway carriage, with her back to the rivers and the sea. Naturally, in a place of that kind, they could not get away without being seen by some of their neighbours. Captain Pentreath was going to Bodmin, and insisted upon throwing away a half-finished cigar in order to enjoy the privilege of Colonel and Mrs. Disney's society, being one of those unmeditative animals who hate solitude. He talked all the way to Par, lit a fresh cigar during the wait at the junction, and re-appeared just as the colonel and his wife were taking their seats in the up-train.

"Have you room for me in there?" he asked, sacrificing more than half of his second cigar. "I've got the *Mercury*—Jepps is in for Stokumpton—a great triumph for our side."

He spread out the paper, and made believe to begin to read with a great show of application, as if he meant to devour every syllable of Jepps's long exposition of the political situation; but after two minutes he dropped the *Mercury* on his knees and began to talk. There were people in Fowey who doubted whether Captain Pentreath could read. He had been able once, of course, or he could hardly have squeezed himself into the Army; but there was an idea that he had forgotten the accomplishment, except in its most elementary form upon sign-boards, and in the headings of newspaper articles, printed large. It was supposed that the intensity of effort by which he had taken in the cramming that enabled him to pass the ordeal of the Examiners had left his brain a blank.

"You're not going further than Plymouth, I suppose?" he asked.

"We are going to London."

"Are you really, now? A bad time of year

for London—fogs and thaws, and all kinds of beastly weather."

And then he asked a string of questions—futile, trivial, vexing as summer flies buzzing round the head of an afternoon sleeper; and then came the welcome cry of Bodmin Road, and he reluctantly left them.

The rest of the journey was passed almost in silence. They had the compartment to themselves for the greater part of the time, and they sat in opposite corners, pretending to read—Isola apparently absorbed in a book that she had taken up at random just before she started, when the carriage was at the door, and while Allegra was calling to her to make haste.

It was Carlyle's "Hero Worship." The big words, the magnificent sentences, passed before her eyes like a procession of phantoms. She had not the faintest idea what she was reading; but she followed the lines and turned the leaf at the bottom of a page mechanically.

Martin Disney applied himself to the newspapers which he had accumulated along the line—some at Par, some at Plymouth, some at Exeter, till the compartment was littered all over with them. He turned and tossed them about one after the other. Never had they seemed so empty—the leaders such mere beating the air; the hard facts so few and insignificant. He glanced at Isola as she sat in her corner, motionless and composed. He watched the slender, white hands turning the leaves of her book at regular intervals.

"Is your book very interesting?" he asked, at last, exasperated by her calmness.

He had been attentive and polite to her, offering her the papers, ordering tea for her at Exeter, doing all that a courteous husband ought .to do; but he had made no attempt at conversation—nor had she. This question about the book was wrung from him by the intensity of his irritation.

"It is a book you gave me years ago at Dinan," she answered, looking at him piteously. "'Hero Worship.' Don't you remember? I had never read anything of Carlyle's before then. You taught me to like him."

"Did I? Yes, I remember—a little Tauchnitz volume, bound in morocco—contraband in England. A cheat—like many things in this life."

He turned his face resolutely to the window, as if to end the conversation, and he did not speak again till they were moving slowly into the great station, in the azure brightness of the electric light.

"I have telegraphed for rooms at Whitley's," he said, naming a small private hotel near Cavendish Square where they had stayed for a few days before he started for the East. "Do you think it would be too late for us to call at Hans Place before we go to our hotel?"

She started at the question. He saw her cheeks crimson in the lamplight.

"I don't think the lateness of hour will matter," she said, "unless Gwendoline is dining out. She dines out very often."

"I hope to-night may be an exception."

"Do you want very much to see her?" asked Isola.

"Very much."

"You are going to question her about me, I suppose?"

"Yes, Isola, that is what I am going to do."

"It is treating me rather like a criminal; or, at any rate, like a person whose word cannot be believed."

"I can't help myself, Isola. The agony of doubt that I have gone through can only be set at rest in one way. It is so strange a thing, so impossible as it seems to me, that you should have visited your sister while I was away, although no letter I received from you contained the slightest allusion to that visit—an important event in such a monotonous life as yours—and although no word you have ever spoken since my return has touched upon it; till all at once, at a moment's notice, when I tell you of your journey from London and the slander to which it gave occasion—all at once you spring this visit upon me, as if I ought to have known all about it."

"You can ask Gwendoline as many questions as you like," answered Isola, with an offended air, "and you will see if she denies that I went to see her in the December you were away."

Colonel Disney handed his wife into a station brougham. The two portmanteaux were put upon the roof, and the order was given—99, Hans Place—for albeit Mr. Hazelrigg's splendid mansion was described on his cards and his writing-paper as The Towers, it is always as

well to have a number for the commonality to
know us by.

No word was spoken in the long drive by
Park Lane and Knightsbridge, and the seemingly interminable Sloane Street; no word when
the neat little brougham drew up in front of
a lofty flight of steps leading up to a Heidelberg
doorway, set in the midst of a florid red-brick
house, somewhat narrow in proportion to its
height, and with over much ornament in the way
of terra cotta panelling, bay and oriel, balcony
and niche.

A footman in dark green livery and rice
powder opened the door. Mrs. Hazelrigg was at
home. He led the way to one of those dismal
rooms which are to be found in most fine houses
—a room rarely used by the family—a kind of
pound for casual visitors. Sometimes the pound
is as cold and cheerless as a vestry in a new
Anglican church; sometimes it affects a learned
air, lines its walls with books that no one ever
reads, and calls itself a library. Whatever form
or phase it may take, it never fails to chill the
visitor.

There was naturally no fire in this apartment.

Isola sank shivering into a slippery leather chair, near the Early English fender; her husband walked up and down the narrow floor space. This lasted for nearly ten minutes, when Gwendoline came bursting in, a vision of splendour, in a gray plush tea-gown, frothed with much foam of creamy lace and pale pink ribbon, making a cascade of fluffiness from chin to slippered toes.

"What a most astonishing thing!" she cried, after kissing Isola, and holding out both her plump, white hands to the colonel. "Have you dear, good people dropped from the clouds? I thought you were nearly three hundred miles away when the man came to say you were waiting to see me. It is a miracle we are dining at home to-night. We are so seldom at home. Of course you will stay and dine with us. Come up to my room and take off your hat, Isa. No, you needn't worry about dress," anticipating Disney's refusal; "we are quite alone. I am going to dine in my tea-gown, and Daniel is only just home from the city."

"You are very kind; no, my dear Mrs. Hazelrigg, we won't dine with you to-night," answered

Disney. "We have only just come up to town. We drove across the park to see you before going to our hotel. Our portmanteaux are waiting at the door. We are in town for so short a time that I wanted to see you at once—particularly as I have—a rather foolish question to ask you."

His voice grew husky, though he tried his uttermost to maintain a lightness of tone.

"Ask away," said Gwendoline, straightening herself in her glistening grey gown, a splendid example of modern elegance in dress and demeanour, and altogether a more brilliant and imposing beauty than the pale, fragile figure sitting in a drooping attitude beside the fireless hearth. "Ask away," repeated Gwendoline, gaily, glancing at her sister's mournful face as she spoke. "If I can answer you I will—but please to consider that I have a wretched memory."

"You are not likely to forget the fact I want to ascertain. My wife and I have had an argument about dates—we are at variance about the date of her last visit to you—while I was away —and I should like to settle our little dispute, though it did not go so far as a wager. When was she with you? On what date did she leave you?"

All hesitation and huskiness were gone from manner and voice. He stood like a pillar, with his face turned towards his sister-in-law, his eyes resolute and inquiring.

"Oh, don't ask me about dates," cried Gwendoline, "I never know dates. I buy Letts in every form, year after year—but I never can keep up my diary. Nothing but a self-acting diary would be of any use to me. It was in December she came to me—and in December she left—after a short visit. Come, Isa. You must remember the dates of your arrival and departure, better than I. You don't live in the London whirl. You don't have your brains addled by hearing about Buenos Ayres, Reading and Philadelphias, Berthas, Brighton A's, and things."

Martin Disney looked at her searchingly. Her manner was perfectly easy and natural, of a childlike transparency. Her large, bright, blue eyes looked at him—fearless and candid as the eyes of a child.

"You ought to remember that it was on the last day of the year I left this house," said Isola, in her low, depressed voice, as of one weary unto death. "You said enough about it at the time."

"Did I? Oh, I am such a feather-head, *une vraie tête de linotte*, as they used to call me at Dinan. So it was, New Year's Eve—and I was vexed with you for not staying to see the New Year in. That was it. I remember everything about it now."

"Thank you, Mrs. Hazelrigg," said Martin Disney, and then going over to his wife, he said gravely, "Forgive me, Isola, I was wrong."

He held out his hands to her with a pleading look, and she rose slowly from her chair, and let her head fall upon his breast as he put his arms round her, soothing and caressing her.

"My poor girl, I was wrong—wrong—wrong— a sinner against your truth and purity," he murmured low in her ear; and then he added laughingly, to Gwendoline, "Were we not fools to dispute about such a trifle?"

"All married people are fools on occasion," answered Mrs. Hazelrigg. "I have often quar- relled desperately with Daniel about a mere nothing—not because he was wrong, but because I wanted to quarrel. That kind of thing clears the air—like a thunderstorm. One feels so dutiful and affectionate afterwards. Dan gave me this sapphire ring after one of our biggest rows," she added, holding up a sparkling finger.

Daniel Hazelrigg came into the room while she was talking of him, a large man, with a bald head and sandy beard, a genial-looking man, pleased with a world in which he had been permitted always to foresee the rise and fall of stocks. The Hazelriggs were the very type of a comfortable couple, so steeped in prosperity and the good things of this world as to be hardly aware of any keener air outside the gardenia-scented atmosphere of their own house; hardly aware of men who dined badly or women who made their own gowns; much less of men who never dined at all, or women who flung themselves despairing from the parapets of the London bridges.

Mr. Hazelrigg came into the room beaming, looked at his wife and smiled, as he held out his hand to Colonel Disney, looked at his sister-in-law and smiled again, and held out his hand to her, the smile broadening a little as if with really affectionate interest.

"I'm very glad to see you, my dear Mrs. Disney; but I can't compliment you upon looking as well as you did when we last met."

"She is tired after her long journey," said Gwendoline, quickly. "That's all there is amiss."

"The sooner we get to our hotel the better for both of us," said Disney. "We are dusty and weather-beaten, and altogether bad company. Good night, Mrs. Hazelrigg."

"But surely you'll stop and dine; it's close upon eight," remonstrated Hazelrigg, who was the essence of hospitality. "You can send on your luggage, and go to your hotel later."

"You are very good, but we are not fit for dining out. Isola looks half dead with fatigue," answered Disney. "Once more, good night."

He shook hands with husband and wife and hurried Isola to the door.

"Be sure you come to me the first thing to-morrow," said Gwendoline to her sister. "I shall stay in till you come, and I can drive you anywhere you want to go for your shopping —Stores, Lewis and Allenby's—anywhere. I want to show you my drawing-room. I have changed everything in it. You'll hardly know it again."

She and her husband followed the departing guests to the hall, saw them get into the little brougham and drive off into the night; and then Gwendoline put her arm through her husband's with a soft clinging affectionateness, as of a Persian cat, that knew when it was well housed and taken good care of.

"Poor Isa! how awfully ill she looks," sighed Gwendoline.

"Ghastly. Are all women alike, I wonder, Gwen ? "

"I think you ought to know what kind of woman I am by this time," retorted his wife, tossing up her head.

Martin Disney and his wife were alone in their sitting-room at the hotel, somewhat bare and unhomelike, as all hotel rooms must always be, despite the march of civilization which has introduced certain improvements. He had made a pretence of dining in the coffee-room below, and she had taken some tea and toast beside the fire; and now at ten o'clock they were sitting on each side of the hearth, face to face, pale and thoughtful, and strangely silent.

"Isola, have you forgiven me?" he asked at last.

"With all my heart. Oh, Martin, I could never be angry with you—never. You have been so good to me. How could I be angry?"

"But you have the right to be angry. I ought not to have doubted. I ought to have believed your word against all the world; but that man raised a doubting devil in me. I was mad with fears and suspicions, wild and unreasonable—as I suppose jealousy generally is. I had never been jealous before. Great God! what a fearful passion it is when a man gives himself up to it. I frightened you by my vehemence, and then your scared looks frightened me. I mistook fear for guilt. Isola, my beloved, let me hear the truth from your own lips—the assurance—the certainty," he cried with impassioned fervour, getting up and going over to her, looking down into the pale, upturned face with those dark, earnest eyes which always seemed to search the mysteries of her heart.

"Let there be no shadow of uncertainty or distrust between us. I have heard from your sister that you were with her when you said you were. That is much. It settles for that vile cad's insinuated slander; but it is not enough. Let the assurance come to me from your lips—from yours alone. Tell me—by the God who will judge us both some day—Are you my own true wife?"

"I am, Martin—I am your own true wife," she answered, with an earnestness that thrilled him. "I have not a thought that is not of you. I love you with all my heart and mind. Is not that enough?"

"Yes, yes. And you have never wronged me? You have been true and pure always? I call upon God to hear your words, Isola. Is that true?"

"Yes, yes; it is true."

"God bless you, darling! I will never speak of doubt again. You are my own sweet wife, and shall be honoured and trusted to the end of my days. Thank God, the cloud is past, and we can be happy again!"

She rose from her low seat by the fire, and

put her arms round his neck, and hid her face upon his breast, sobbing hysterically.

"My own dear girl, I have been cruel to you —brutal and unkind; but you would forgive me if you knew what I have suffered since noon yesterday; and, indeed, my suffering began before then. That man's harping on Lostwithiel's name in all his talk with you—his manner of meaning more than he said—and your embarrassment, awakened suspicions that had to be set at rest somehow. Remember the disadvantages under which I labour—the difference in our ages; my unattractiveness as compared with younger men. These things predisposed me to doubt your love. I have not had a moment's peace since the night of that odious dinner-party. Yes; I have felt a new sensation. I know what jealousy means. But it is past. Praise be to God, it is past. I have come out of the cloud again. Oh, my love, had it been otherwise! Had we been doomed to part!"

"What would you have done, Martin?" she asked, in a low voice, with her face still hidden against his breast, his arms still round her.

"What would I have done, love? Nothing to bring shame on you. Nothing to add to your dishonour or sharpen the agony of remorse. I should have taken my son—my son could not be left under the shadow of a mother's shame. He and I would have vanished out of your life. You would have heard no more of us. The world would have known nothing. You would have been cared for and protected from further evil—protected from your own frailty. So far, I would have done my duty as your husband to the last day of my life; but you and I would never have looked upon each other again."

Colonel Disney and his wife stayed in London two days; perhaps to give a colour to their sudden and in somewise unexplained journey; but Isola refused all her sister's invitations, to lunch, to drive, to dine, to go to an afternoon concert at the Albert Hall, or to see the last Shakespearean revival at the Lyceum. She pleaded various excuses; and Gwendoline had to be satisfied with one visit, at afternoon tea-time, when husband and wife appeared together, on the eve of their return to Cornwall.

"It was too bad of you not to come to me yesterday morning, as you promised," Gwendoline said to her sister. "I stayed indoors till after luncheon on your account; and the days are so short at this time of year. I couldn't do any shopping."

Mrs. Hazelrigg was one of those young women for whom life is flavourless when they have nothing to buy. She was so well supplied with everything that women desire or care for that she had to invent wants for herself. She had to watch the advertisements in order to tempt herself with some new wish; were it only for a patent toast-rack, or a new design in ivory paper-knives. The stationers helped to keep life in her by their new departures in writing-paper. Papyrus, Mandarin, Telegraphic, Good Form, Casual, mauve, orange, scarlet, verdigris green. So long as the thing was new it made an excuse for shopping.

"You never came to look at my drawing-room by daylight," she went on complainingly. "You can't possibly judge the tints by lamp-light. Every chair is of a different shade. I think you have treated me shamefully. I have sent you more telegrams than I could count. And I had such lots to talk about. Have you heard from Dinan lately?"

"Not since August, when mother wrote in answer to our invitation for her and father to spend a month with us. I felt it was hopeless when I wrote to her."

"Utterly hopeless! Nothing will tempt her to cross the sea. She writes about it as if it were the Atlantic. And Lucy Folkestone tells me she is getting stouter."

" You mean mother ?"

"Yes, naturally. There's no fear of Lucy ever being anything but bones. Mother is stouter and more sedentary than ever, Lucy says. It's really dreadful. One doesn't know where it will end," added Gwendoline, looking down at her own somewhat portly figure, as if foreseeing hereditary evil.

"I shall have to take Isa and the boy to Dinan next summer," said Disney. "It is no use asking the father and mother to cross the channel ; though I think they would both like to see their grandson."

"Mother raved about him in her last letter to

me," replied Gwendoline. " She was quite overcome by the photograph you sent her, only she
has got into such a groove—her knitting, her
novel, her little walk on the terrace, her long
consultations with Manette about the smallest
domestic details—whether the mattresses shall
be unpicked to-day or to-morrow, or whether the
lessive shall be a week earlier or a week later.
It is dreadful to think of such a life," added
Gwendoline, as if her own existence were one of
loftiest aims.

CHAPTER III.

"SORROW THAT'S DEEPER THAN WE DREAM,
PERCHANCE."

LIFE flowed on its monotonous course, always more or less like the Fowey river gliding down from Lostwithiel to the sea; and there seemed nothing in this world that could again disturb Martin Disney's domestic peace. Vansittart Crowther made no further attempt to avenge himself for the night attack upon his gates; nor did he demand any apology for the vulgar abuse which he had suffered in the sanctuary of his own library. This he endured, and even further outrage, in the shape of the following letter from Colonel Disney :—

"SIR,

"As you have been pleased to take a certain old-womanish interest in my domestic affairs, I think it may be as well to satisfy your curiosity so far as to inform you that when your solicitor travelled in the same train with my wife, she was returning from a visit to her married sister's house, a visit which had my sanction and approval. I can only regret that her husband's modest means constrained her to travel alone, and subjected her to the impertinent attentions of one cad and to the slanderous aspersions of another.

"I have the honour to be,

"Yours, etc.,

"MARTIN DISNEY."

Mr. Crowther treated this letter with the silent contempt which he told himself it merited. What could he say to a man so possessed by uxorious hallucinations, so steeped in the poppy and mandragora of a blind affection, that reason had lost all power over his mind.

"I spoke plain enough—as plain as I dared," said Mr. Crowther. "He may ride the high horse and bluster as much as he likes. I don't think he'll ever feel quite happy again."

Yet in spite of hints and insinuations from

the enemy at his gates, Martin Disney was happy—utterly happy in the love of his young wife, and in the growing graces of his infant son. He no longer doubted Isola's affection. Her tender regard for him showed itself in every act of her life; in every look of the watchful face that was always on the alert to divine his pleasure, to forestall his wishes. Mrs. Baynham went about everywhere expatiating on the domestic happiness of the Disney family, to whom she was more than ever devoted, now that she felt herself in a manner related to them, having been elevated to the position of god-mother to the firstborn—a very different thing to being godmother to some sixth or seventh link in the family-chain, when all thought of selection has been abandoned, and the only question mooted by the parents has been, "Whom can we ask this time?"

Captain Hulbert took his yacht to other waters in November, only to come sailing back again in December, when he finally laid up the *Vendetta* in winter quarters, and took up his abode at the Mount, where he availed himself of his brother's stud, which had been fined down to two old hunters and a pair of carriage-horses of mediocre quality. And so the shortening days drew on towards Christmas; baby's first Christmas, as that small person's adorers remarked—as if it were a wonderful thing for any young Christian to make a beginning of life—and all was happiness at the Angler's Nest. All was happiness without a cloud, till one morning—Allegra and her brother being alone in the library, where she sometimes painted at her little table-easel, while he read— she put down her palette and went over to him, laying her hand upon his shoulder as he sat in his accustomed place in the old-fashioned bow-window.

"Martin, I want to speak to you about Isola," she said, rather tremulously.

"What about her? Why she was here this minute," he exclaimed. "Is there anything amiss?"

"I do not think she is so strong as she ought to be. You may not notice, perhaps. A woman is quicker to see these things than a man—and she and I used to walk and row together—I am able to see the difference in her since last year.

She seems to me to have been going back in her health for the last month or two, since her wonderful recovery from her illness. Don't be anxious, Martin!" she said, answering his agonized look. " I feel sure there is nothing that a little care cannot cure; but I want to put you on your guard. I asked her to let me send for Mr. Baynham, and she refused."

" Why, he sees her two or three times a week —he is in and out like one of ourselves."

" But he doesn't see her professionally. He comes in hurriedly late in the evening—or between the lights—to fetch his wife. He is tired, and we all talk to him, and Isa is bright and lively. He is not likely to notice the change in her in that casual way."

" Is there a change ? "

" Yes, I am sure there is. Although I see her every day, I am conscious of the change."

" Baynham shall talk to her this afternoon."

" That's right, Martin—and if I were you I'd have the doctor from Plymouth again."

Life had been so full of bliss lately, and yet he had not been afraid. Yes, it was the old story. " Metuit secundis." That is what the wise man does. Fools do otherwise—hug themselves in their short-lived gladness, and say in their hearts, "There is no death."

Mr. Baynham came in the afternoon, in answer to a little note from Martin Disney, and he and Isola were closeted together in the library for some time, with baby's nurse in attendance to assist her mistress in preparing for the ordeal by stethoscope. Happily that little instrument which thrills us all with the aching pain of fear when we see it in the doctor's hand, told no evil tidings of Isola's lungs or heart. There was nothing organically wrong—but the patient was in a very weak state.

"You really are uncommonly low," said Mr. Baynham, looking at her intently as she stood before him in the wintry sunlight. "I don't know what you've been doing to yourself to bring yourself down so much since last summer —after all the trouble I took to build you up, too. I'm afraid you've been worrying yourself about the youngster—a regular young Hercules. I don't know whether he'd be up to strangling a pair of prize pythons; but I'm sure he could strangle you. I shall send you a tonic; and you'll have to take a good deal more care of yourself than you seem to have been taking lately."

And then he laid down severe rules as to diet, until it seemed to Isola that he wished her to be eating and drinking all day—new laid eggs, cream, old port, beef tea—all the things which she had loathed in the dreary days of her long illness in May and June.

Mr. Baynham had a serious talk with the colonel after he left Isola, and it was agreed between them that she should be taken to Plymouth next day to see the great authority.

"You are taking a great deal too much trouble about me, Martin," she said. "There is nothing wrong. I am only a little weak and tired sometimes."

Her husband looked at her heart-brokenly. Weak and tired. Yes; there were all the signs of failing life in those languid movements of the long, slender limbs, in the transparent pallor of the ethereal countenance. Decay was lovely in this fair young form; but he felt that it was decay. There must be something done to stop Misfortune's hastening feet.

He questioned his wife, he questioned his own memory, as to when the change had begun, and on looking back thus thoughtfully it seemed to him that her spirits and her strength had flagged from the time of Captain Hulbert's arrival at Fowey. She had seemed tolerably cheerful until then, interested in life, ready to participate in any amusement or occupation of Allegra's; but from the beginning of their yachting excursions there had been a change. She had shrunk from any share in their plans or expeditions. She had gone on board the yacht—on the two or three occasions when she had been persuaded to go— with obvious reluctance, and she had been silent and joyless all the time she was there. Within the last fortnight, when Captain Hulbert had pressed her to go to luncheon or afternoon tea at the Mount, she had persistently refused. She had begged her husband to take Allegra, and to excuse her.

"The walk up the hill would tire me," she said.

"My love, why should we walk? I will drive you there, of course."

"I really had rather not go. I can't bear

leaving baby so long; and there is no necessity for me to be with you. Allegra is the person who is wanted. You must understand that, Martin. You can see how much Captain Hulbert admires her."

"And I am to go and do gooseberry while you do baby-worship at home. Rather hard upon me."

This kind of thing had occurred three or four times since the sailor's establishment at the Mount, and Colonel Disney had attached no significance to the matter; but now that he had begun to torture himself by unending speculations upon the cause of her declining health, he could but think that Captain Hulbert's society had been distasteful to her. It might be that Mr. Crowther's insulting allusions to Lord Lostwithiel had made any association with that name painful; and yet this would seem an overstrained sensitiveness, since her own innocence of all evil should have made her indifferent to a vulgarian's covert sneers.

CHAPTER IV.

"THE YEAR OF THE ROSE IS BRIEF."

MR. BAYNHAM accompanied his patient and her husband to Plymouth, where the family adviser of Trelasco had a long and serious talk with the leading medical light of the great seaport. The result of which consultation—after the tossing to and fro of such words as anæmia, atrophy, family history, hysteria, between the two doctors, as lightly as if diseases were shuttle-cocks—was briefly communicated to Colonel Disney in a sentence that struck terror to his heart, carefully as it was couched. It amounted in plain words to this: We think your wife's condition serious enough to cause alarm, although there are at present no indications of organic disease. Should her state of bodily weakness and mental depression continue, we apprehend atrophy, or perhaps chronic hysteria.

Under these circumstances, we strongly recommend you to give her a change of scene, and a milder winter climate even than that of the west of England. Were she living in Scotland or Yorkshire we might send her to Fowey; but as it is we should advise either a sea voyage, or a residence for the rest of the winter at Pau, Biarritz, or on the Riviera.

Modern medicine has a high-handed way of sending patients to the uttermost ends of the earth; and although Martin Disney thought with a regretful pang of the house and stables that he had built and beautified for himself, the garden where every shrub was dear, yet he felt grateful to the specialist for not ordering him to take his wife to the banks of the Amazon or to some remote valley in Cashmere. Pau is not far —the Riviera is the beaten track of civilized Europe, the highway road to Naples and the East. He thought of the happy honeymoon, when he and his bright young wife had travelled along that garden of oranges and lemons, between the hills and the sea, and how there had been no shadow on their lives except the shadow of impending separation, about which

they had talked hopefully, trying to believe
that a year or two would not seem very long,
trying to project their thoughts into that
happy future when there should be no more
parting.

This—this dreary present—was that future
which they had pictured as a period of unalloyed
bliss. What had the future brought to that
hopeful husband, going forth at the call of duty,
to return with fondest expectations when his
work was done? What but a year and a half
of wedded life overshadowed by disappointment,
darkened by vague doubts? And now came the
awful fear of a longer parting than had lain at
the end of his last Italian journey.

The patient herself was told nothing except
that change to a warmer climate would be good
for her, and that her husband had promised to
take her to the South soon after Christmas.

"You will like to go, won't you, Isola?" he
asked her tenderly, as they drove back to the
station alone, leaving Mr. Baynham to follow his
own devices in the town. "You will enjoy
seeing the places we saw together when our
marriage was still a new thing?"

"I shall like to go anywhere with you, Martin," she answered. "But is it really necessary to go away? I know you love Trelasco."

"Oh, I have the Cornishman's passion for his native soil; but I am not so rooted to it as to pine in exile. I shall be happy enough in the South, with my dear young wife; especially if I see the roses come back to your cheeks in that land of roses."

"But it will cost you such a lot of money to take us all away, Martin; and you could not leave Allegra or the baby. Doctors have such expensive ideas."

"Allegra, and the boy! Must we take them, do you think, love?"

"We could not leave him," said Isola, horrified at the bare suggestion; "and it would be very hard to leave Allegra. She bore all the burden of my illness. She has been so good and unselfish. And she will so revel in the South. She has never travelled, she, for whom Nature means so much more than it can for you or me."

"Well, we will take Allegra, and the boy, whose railway ticket will cost nothing, and his nurse. There is a shot in the locker still, Isa, in spite of last year's building operations, which cost a good deal more than I expected. We will all migrate together. Consider that settled. The only question that remains is the direction in which we shall go. Shall we make for the Pyrenees or the Maritime Alps? Shall we go to Pau, and Biarritz, or to the Riviera, Hyères, Cannes, Nice?"

Isola was in favour of Pau, but after much consultation of books recording other people's experiences, it was finally decided that of all places in the world, San Remo was the best winter home for Isola Disney.

"You can take her up to the Engadine in June," said Mr. Baynham, who had a superficial familiarity with the Continent from hearing his patients talk about their travels, he himself never having left Cornwall, except for a plunge into the metropolitan vortex during the Cattle Show week. "Or you may spend your summer in Auvergne—unless you want to come home as soon as the cold weather is over."

"I shall do whatever may be best for her—home or otherwise," answered Disney. "You may be sure of that."

The doctor went back to his wife, with whom he always discussed everything, except purely professional matters—there were even occasions when he could not refrain from enlarging upon the interesting features of some very pretty case —and was enthusiastic in his praise of Martin Disney.

"I never saw such devotion," he said. "Any other man would think it hard lines to have to strike his tent at a day's notice, and go off to winter at a strange place, among invalids and old women; but Disney says never a word of his own inclinations or his own inconvenience. He positively adores that young woman. I only hope she's worth it."

"She's very fond of him, Tom," replied Mrs. Baynham, decisively. "There was a time when I was rather doubtful about that. She seemed listless and indifferent. But since the baby came she has been growing fonder and fonder of her husband. I flatter myself I am a pretty good judge of countenances, and I can read hers. I've seen her face light up when the colonel came into the room. I've seen her go over to him shyly, as if she were still in her honeymoon. She's a very sweet creature. I took to her from the first; and I shall be dreadfully upset if she goes into a decline."

The doctor shook his head despondently.

"There's nothing to fight with in her case," he said, "and there's very little to fall back upon. I can't make her out. She has gone off just like a girl who was simply fretting herself to death; and yet, if she's fond of her husband, what in Heaven's name is there for her to fret about?"

"Nothing," answered his wife. "It's just a delicate constitution, that's all. She's like one of those grape hyacinths that never will stand upright in a vase. The stem isn't strong enough."

Allegra was all sympathy and affection. She would go with them—yes, to the end of the world. To go to San Remo would be of course delightful.

"It is a deliciously paintable place, I know," she said, "for I have seen bits of the scenery often enough in the exhibitions. I shall work prodigiously, and earn a small fortune."

She told her brother in the most delicate way that she meant to pay her own expenses in this Italian tour; for of course when Isola should be strong enough they would go about a little, and see the Wonderland of Italy.

Martin protested warmly against any such arrangement.

"Then I shall not go," she exclaimed. "Do you think me one of the incapable young women of the old school—unable to earn a sixpence, and wanting to be paid for and taken care of like a child? I would have you to know, sir, that I am one of the young women of the new school, who travel third-class, ride on the tops of omnibuses, and earn their own living."

"But I shall take a house at San Remo, Allegra. Do you expect me to turn innkeeper—charge you for your bed and board?"

"Oh, you are monstrously proud. You can do as you like in your own house, I suppose. But all travelling and hotel expenses will be my affair, remember that."

"And you don't mind leaving Trelasco?"

"I am like Ruth. You are my home and my country. Where thou goest I will go."

"And Captain Hulbert—how will he like to lose you?"

"What am I to Captain Hulbert?" she asked,

trying to laugh off the question, but blushing deeply as she bent over her colour-box, suddenly interested in the littered contents.

"A great deal, I fancy, though he may not have found plain speech for his feelings yet awhile."

"If—if you are not a very foolish person, and there is any foundation for your absurd idea, Captain Hulbert will know where to find us. He can spread his wings and follow."

"The *Vendetta?* Yes, she is pretty familiar with the bays and bights of the Mediterranean. No doubt he will follow us, dear. But I should like him to speak out before we go."

"Then I'm afraid you will be disappointed. He likes coming here—he likes you and Isola, and perhaps he likes me, pretty well, after a fashion; but sailors are generally fickle, are they not? And if he is at all like his brother, Lord Lostwithiel, who seems to have a dreadful reputation, judging by the way people talk of him here——"

"He is not like his brother in character or disposition. If he were, I should be sorry for my sister to marry him."

"Have you such a very bad opinion of his brother?" asked Allegra, shocked and grieved that any one closely allied to John Hulbert should bear an evil repute.

"Perhaps that would be too much to say. I know so little about him. I have scarcely seen him since he was a lad—only I have heard things which have prejudiced me," continued Disney, lapsing into moody thoughtfulness.

Was it not Mr. Crowther's insolence, and that alone, which had prejudiced him against Lostwithiel—had made the very name hateful to him? Yes, that was the cause of his aversion. He had disproved those insolent insinuations; he had exploded the covert slander and rebuked the slanderer; but he had not forgotten. The wound still rankled.

CHAPTER V.

"NO SUDDEN FANCY OF AN ARDENT BOY."

IT was Christmas Eve. All things were arranged for departure on the 28th, which would give time for their arrival at San Remo on New Year's Day. They were to travel by easy stages, by Amiens, Basle, and Lucerne. A good deal of luggage had been sent off in advance, and trunks and portmanteaux were packed ready for the start; so that the travellers could take their ease during the few days of Christmas church-going and festivity. Isola's spirits had improved wonderfully since the journey had been decided upon.

"It seems like beginning a new life, Martin," she told her husband. "I feel ever so much better already. I'm afraid I'm an impostor, and that you are taking a great deal of unnecessary trouble on my account."

It was such a relief to think that she would see Vansittart Crowther no more, that she could wander where she pleased without the hazard of meeting that satyr-like countenance, those pale protruding eyes, with malevolent stare—such a relief to know that she would be in a new country, where no one would know anything about her, or have any inclination to gossip about her. Something of her old gaiety and interest in life revived at the prospect of those new surroundings.

They were to put up at an hotel for the first few days, so as to take their time in looking for a villa. Two servants were to go with them— the colonel's valet and handy-man, who was an old soldier, and could turn his hand to anything in house, or stable, or garden; and the baby's nurse, a somewhat masterful person of seven and twenty, from the Fatherland, surnamed Grunhaupt, but known in the family by her less formidable domestic diminutive Löttchen. Other hirelings would be obtained at San Remo, but these two were indispensable— Holford, the soldier-servant, to bear all burdens, and Löttchen to take charge of the baby, to whom life was supposed to be impossible in any other care.

It was Christmas Eve—the mildest Christmas that had been known for a long time, even in this sheltered corner of the coast. Allegra had been busy all the morning, helping in the church decorations, and co-operating with Mr. Colfox in various arrangements for the comfort of the very old and feeble, and the invalids, among the cottages scattered over the length and breadth of a large parish. She had walked a good many miles, and she had stood for an hour in the church, toiling at the decoration of the font, ferns, arbutus, and berberis foliage, in all their varieties of colour, from darkest bronze to vivid crimson, starred with the whiteness of Christmas roses; while the Miss Crowthers lavished the riches of the Glenaveril hot-houses upon the pulpit, keeping themselves studiously aloof from Miss Leland.

Not a jot cared Allegra for their aloofness. She disliked their father, and she knew that her brother detested him, without having any clear idea of the cause. She was so thoroughly loyal to Martin that she would have deemed it treason to like any one whom he disliked; so had the daughters of Glenaveril been the most lovable young women in Cornwall she would have considered it her duty to hold them at arm's length. Glenaveril and all its belongings were taboo.

She was very tired when she went home at four o'clock, just on the edge of dusk here— pitch dark, no doubt, in London and other great cities, where the poor, pinched faces were flitting to and fro in the fitful glare of the gas, intent on buying a Christmas dinner to fit the slenderest resources.   Here, in this quiet valley, the re- flected sun-glow still brightened sky, sea, land, and river, and the lamps had not yet been lighted in hall or drawing-room at the Angler's Nest.

There was a pleasant alternation of firelight and shadow in the long double room, the flames leaping up every now and then, and lighting wall and bookcase, picture and bust, the blue and red of the Mandarin jars, and the golden storks on the black Japanese screen; but it was such a capricious light that it did not show Allegra some one sitting *perdu* in Martin Disney's deep elbow chair, a person who sat and watched her with an admiring smile, as she flung off her little felt hat and fur cape, and stretched her arms above her head in sheer weariness, a graceful, picturesque figure, in her plain brown serge gown, belted round the supple waist, and clasped at the throat, like Enid's, and with never an ornament except the oxydized silver clasps, and the serviceable chatelaine hanging at her side.

The tea-table was set ready in front of the fire, the large Moorish brass tray on bamboo legs. But there was no sign of Isola; so Miss Leland poured out a cup of tea and began to drink it, still unconscious of a pair of dark eyes watching her from the shadow of the big armchair.

"And am I to have no tea, Miss Leland?" asked a voice out of the darkness.

Allegra gave a little scream, and almost dropped her cup.

"Good gracious!" she exclaimed. "How can you startle any one like that? How do you know that I have not heart disease?"

"I would as soon suspect the goddess Hygeia of that, or any other ailment," said Captain Hulbert, rising to his full six feet two, out of the low chair in the dark corner by the bookcase. "Forgive me for my bearishness in sitting here while you were in the room. I could not resist the temptation to sit and watch you for a minute or two while you were unconscious of my presence. It was like looking at a picture. While you are talking I am so intent upon what you say, and what you think, that I almost forget to consider what you are like. To-night I could gaze undistracted."

"What absolute nonsense you talk," said Allegra, with the sugar-tongs poised above the basin. "One lump—or two?"

"One, two, three—anything you like—up to a million."

"Do you know that you nearly made me break a tea-cup—one of mother's dear old Worcester tea-cups? I should never have forgiven you."

"But as you didn't drop the tea-cup, I hope you do forgive me for my stolen contemplation, for sitting in my corner there and admiring you in the firelight?"

"Firelight is very becoming. No doubt I looked better than in the daytime."

"And you forgive me?"

"I suppose so. It is hardly worth while to be

angry with you. I shall be a thousand miles away next week. I could not carry my resentment so far. It would cool on the journey."

"A thousand miles is not far for the *Vendetta,* Miss Leland. She would make light of crossing the Pacific—for a worthy motive."

"I don't know anything about motives; but I thought you were fairly established at the Mount, and that you had made an end of your wanderings."

"The Mount is only delightful—I might say endurable—when I have neighbours at the Angler's Nest."

"Martin will let this house, perhaps, and you may have pleasant neighbours in the new people."

"I am not like the domestic cat. It is not houses I care for, but individuals. My affections would not transfer themselves to the new tenants."

"How can you tell that? You think of them to-night as strangers—and they seem intolerable. You would like them after a week, and be warmly attached to them at the end of a month. Why, you have known us for less than three months, and we fancy ourselves quite old friends."

"Oh, Miss Leland, is our friendship only fancy? Will a thousand miles make you forget me?"

"No, we could not any of us be so ungrateful as to forget you," answered Allegra, struggling against growing embarrassment, wondering if this tender tone, these vague nothings, were drifting towards a declaration, or were as simply meaningless as much of the talk between men and women. "We can't forget how kind you have been, and what delightful excursions we have had on the *Vendetta*."

"The *Vendetta* will be at San Remo when you want her, Allegra. She will be as much at your command there as she has been here; and her skipper will be as much your slave as he is here—as he has been almost ever since he saw your face."

This was not small talk. This meant something very serious. He had called her Allegra, and she had not reproved him; he had taken her hand and she had not withdrawn it. In the next instant, she knew not how, his arm was round her waist, and her head, weary with the long day's work and anxieties, was resting contentedly on his shoulder, while his lips set their first kiss, tenderly, reverently almost, on her fair broad brow.

"Allegra, this means yes, does it not? Our lives have flowed on together so peacefully, so happily, since last October. They are to mingle and flow on together to the great sea, are they not, love—the sea of death and eternity."

"Do you really care for me?"

"Do I really adore you? Yes, dear love. With all my power of adoration."

"But you must have cared for other girls before now. I can't believe that I am the first."

"Believe, at least, that you will be the last, as you are the only woman I ever asked to be my wife."

"Is that really, really true?"

"It is true as the needle to the north."

"Yet they say that sailors——"

"Are generally tolerable dancers, and popular in a ball-room, especially when they are the givers of the ball—that they can talk to pretty women without feeling abashed—and that they contrive to get through a good deal of flirting without singeing their wings. I have waltzed with a good many nice girls in my time, Allegra, and I have sat out a good many waltzes. Yet I am here at your side, honestly and devotedly your own; and I have never loved any other woman with the love I feel for you. No other woman has ever held my whole heart; no, not for a single hour."

"You make nice distinctions," said Allegra, gently disengaging herself from his arm, and looking at him with a faint, shy smile, very doubtful, yet very anxious to believe. "I am dreadfully afraid that all this fine talk means nothing more than you would say to any of your partners, if you happened to be sitting out a waltz."

"Should I ask any of my partners to be my wife, do you think?"

"Oh, you can withdraw that to-morrow—forget and ignore it. We may both consider it only a kind of under-the-mistletoe declaration, meaning no more than a mistletoe kiss. I believe when English people were domestic and kept Christmas, the head of the family would have kissed his cook if he had met her under the mistletoe."

" Allegra, is it not cruel of you to be jocose when I am so tremendously serious? "

" What if I don't believe in your seriousness?"

" Is this only a polite way of refusing me ? " he asked, beginning to be offended, not understanding that this nonsense-talk was a hasty defence against overpowering emotion, that she was not sure of him, and was desperately afraid of betraying herself. " Am I to understand that you don't care a straw for me ? "

" No, no, no," she cried eagerly, " as a friend, I like you better than any one else in the world; only I don't want to give you more than friendship till I can trust you well enough to believe in your love."

" Prove it, Allegra," he cried, clasping her waist again before she was aware. " Put me to any test or any trial—impose any duty upon me. Only tell me that if I come through the ordeal you will be my wife."

" You are not in a great hurry to fetter yourself, I hope ? " she said.

"I am in a hurry—I long for those sweet fetters by which your love will hold me. I want to be anchored by my happiness."

"Give me a year of freedom, a year for art and earnest work in Italy, a year for Martin and Isola, who both want me; and if this night year you are still of the same mind, I will be your wife. I will not engage you. You may be as free as air to change your mind and love some one else; but I will promise to be true to you and to this talk of ours till the year's end—one year from to-night."

"I accept your sentence, though it is severe; but I don't accept my freedom. I am your slave for a year. I shall be your slave when the year is out. I am yours, and yours alone for life. And now give me that cup of tea, Allegra, which you have not poured out yet, and let us fancy ourselves Darby and Joan."

"Darby and Joan," echoed Allegra, as she filled his cup. "Must we be like that, old and prosy, sitting by the fire, while life goes by us outside? It seems sad that there should be no alternative between old age and untimely death."

"It is sad; but the world is made so. And

then Providence steeps elderly people in a happy hallucination. They generally forget that they are old; or at least they forget that they ever were young, and they think young people so ineffably silly that youth itself seems despicable to their sober old minds. But you and I have a long life to the good, dear love, before the coming of grey hairs and elderly prejudices."

And then he began to talk of ways and means, as if they were going to be married next week.

"We shall have enough for bread and cheese, love," he said. "I am better off than a good many younger sons; for a certain old grandmother in our family married with a settlement which provided for the younger branches. It is quite possible that Lostwithiel may never marry—indeed, he seems to me very decided against matrimony, and in that case those who come after us must inherit title and estate in days to come."

"Pray don't talk so," cried Allegra, horrified. "It sounds as if you were speculating upon your brother's death."

"On Lostwithiel's death? Not for worlds. God bless him, wherever he may be. You don't

know how fond we two fellows are of each other.
Only when a man is going to be married it
behoves him to think even of the remote future.
I shall have to talk to the colonel, remember;
and he will expect me to be explicit and
business-like."

"I hope you don't think Martin mercenary,"
said Allegra. "There never was a man who set
less value on money. It wouldn't make any
difference to him if you had not a penny. And
as for me, I have a little income from my mother
—more than enough to buy frocks and things—
and beyond that I can earn my own living. So
you really needn't trouble yourself about me."

There was a touching simplicity in her speech,
mingled with a slight flavour of audacity, as of
an emancipated young woman, which amused her
lover, reminding him of a heroine of Murger's,
or Musset's, a brave little grisette, who was
willing to work hard for the *ménage à deux*, and
who wanted nothing from her lover but love.
He looked into the bright, frank face, radiant in
the fire-glow, and he told himself that this was
just the one woman for whom his heart had kept
itself empty, like a temple waiting for its god,

in all the years of his manhood. And now the temple doors had opened wide, the gates had been lifted up, and the goddess had marched to her place, triumphant and all-conquering.

The clock on the mantelpiece struck six, and the old eight-day clock in the hall followed like a solemn echo. Captain Hulbert started up. "So late! Why, we have been talking for nearly two hours!" he exclaimed, "and I have a budget of letters to write for the night mail. Good-bye, darling—or I'll say *au revoir*, for I'll walk down again after dinner, and get half an hour's chat with Disney, if you don't think it will be too late for me to see him."

"You know he is always pleased to see you— we are not very early people—and this is Christmas Eve. We were to sit round the fire and tell ghost-stories, don't you remember?"

"Of course we were. I shall be here soon after nine, and I shall think over all the grizzly legends I ever heard, as I come down the hill."

He went reluctantly, leaving her standing by the fire, a contemplative figure with downcast eyes. At a little later stage in their engagement no doubt she would have gone with him to the door, or even out to the garden gate, for a lingering parting under the stars—but there was a shyness about them both in this sweet dim beginning of their union, when it was so strange to each to have any claim upon the other.

"How lightly she took the whole business," Captain Hulbert said to himself as he went up the hill. "Yet her voice trembled now and then —and her hand was deadly cold when first I clasped it. I think she loves me. A year,"— snapping his fingers gaily at the stars—"what is a year? A year of bliss if it be mostly spent with her. Besides, long engagements are apt to dwindle. I have seen such engagements— entered on solemnly like ours to-night—shrink to six months, or less. Why should one linger on the threshold of a new life, if one knows it is going to be completely happy?"

The blissful lover had not been gone five minutes when Isola came creeping into the room, and put her arm round Allegra's neck and kissed her flushed cheek.

"Why, Isa, where have you been hiding all this evening?"

"I had fallen asleep in my room, just half an

hour before tea, and when I awoke it was five o'clock, and Löttchen told me you and Captain Hulbert were in the drawing-room. And as I know you two have always so much to talk about, I thought I wouldn't disturb you. So I let Löttchen make tea for me in the nursery, and I stayed there to play with baby. And here you are all in the dark."

"Oh, we had the firelight—Parker forgot to bring the lamp."

"And you forgot to ring for it," said Isola, going over to the bow-window, and drawing back a curtain. "What a lovely sky! Who would think it was Christmas-time?"

The moon was in her second quarter, shining brilliantly, in the deep purple of a sky almost without a cloud.

"Will you put on your hat and jacket and come for a stroll in the garden, Isa?" asked Allegra. "It is a mild, dry night, and I don't think the air can hurt you."

"Hurt me! It will do me all the good in the world. Yes, I shall be ready in a moment."

They went out into the hall, where Allegra packed her sister-in-law carefully in a warm, fur-lined jacket, and flung a tartan shawl round her own shoulders. Then they went out into the garden, and to the lawn by the river. The moon was shining on the running water, brightly, coldly, clear, while the meadows on the opposite bank were wrapped in faint, white mists, which made all the landscape seem unreal.

"Are you not too tired for walking here after your long day, Allegra?" Isola asked, when they had gone up and down the path two or three times.

"Tired, no. I could walk to Tywardreath. I could walk to the Mausoleum. Shall we go there? The sea must be lovely under that moon."

"My dearest, it is nearly seven o'clock, and you have been tramping about all day. If you are not very tired, you must be very much excited, Allegra. I am longing to hear what it all means."

"Are you really, now? Do you care about it, Isola? Can you, who are firmly anchored in the haven of marriage, feel any sentimental interest in other people, tossing about on the sea of courtship? Martin is to be told everything to-night—so you may as well know all about it now. You like Captain Hulbert, don't you, Isola?"

"I do, indeed. I like him, and believe in him."

"Thank Heaven! I should have been miserable if you had doubted or disliked him. He is to be my husband some day, Isa, if Martin approve— but not for a year, at least. Tell me, dear, are you glad?"

"Yes, I am very glad. God bless you, Allegra, and make your life happy—and free—from— care."

She broke down with those last faltered words, and Allegra discovered that she was crying.

"My dearest Isa, don't cry! I shall fancy you are sorry—that you think him unworthy."

"No, no, no. It is not that. He is worthy. He is all that I could desire in the man who is to be your husband. No, I was only thinking how completely happy you and he must be—how cloudless your life promises to be. God keep you, and guard you, dear! And may you never know the pain of parting with the husband you love—with your protector and friend—as I have known it."

"Yes, love; but that is all past and done with. There are to be no more farewells for you and Martin."

"No, it is past, thank God! Yet one cannot forget. I am very glad Captain Hulbert has left the navy—that his profession cannot call him away from you."

"No, he is an idle man. I dare say the time will come when I shall be plagued with him, and be almost obliged to suggest that he should keep race-horses, or go on the Stock Exchange, to occupy his time. I have heard women say that it is terrible to have a stay-at-home husband. Yet Martin is never *de trop*—but then Martin can bury himself in a book. He has no fidgety ways."

"How lightly you talk, Allegra."

"Perhaps that is because my heart is heavy—heavy, not with grief and care, but with the burden of perplexity and surprise, with the fear that comes of a great joy."

"You do love him, then?" said Isola, earnestly. "You are glad."

"I am very glad. I am glad with all my heart."

"God bless you, dearest! I rejoice in your happiness."

They kissed again, this time with tears on both sides; for Allegra was now quite overcome, and sobbed out her emotion upon her sister's neck; they two standing clasped in each other's arms beside the river.

" When I am dead, Allegra, remember always that I loved you, and that I rejoiced in your happiness as if it were my own."

" When you are dead! How dare you talk like that, when we are taking you away to get well and strong, and to live ever so many years beyond your golden wedding? Was there ever such ingratitude?"

The odour of tobacco stole on the evening air, and they heard Martin's firm tread approaching along the gravel path.

Isola put her arm through his, while Allegra ran into the house, and husband and wife walked up and down two or three times in the darkness, she telling him all about the wonderful thing that had happened.

" You are glad, are you not, Martin? You are as glad as I am ? "

"Are you so very glad?"

"Yes, for I know that Allegra loves him, has loved him for a long time."

"Meaning six weeks or so—allowing a fortnight for the process of falling in love. Is that what you call a long time, Isola?"

"Weeks are long sometimes," she answered, slowly, as if her thoughts had wandered into another channel.

"Well, if Allegra is pleased, I suppose I ought to be content," said Disney. "Hulbert seems a fine, frank fellow, and I have never heard anything to his discredit. He was popular in the navy, and was considered a man of marked ability. I dare say people will call him a good match for Allegra, so long as Lostwithiel remains a bachelor."

"No one can be too good for Allegra, and only the best of men can be good enough. If I had my own way, I should have liked her to remain always unmarried, and to care for nothing but her nephew and you. I should have liked to think of her as always with you by-and-by."

The triangular dinner-party was gayer that evening than it had been for a long time. Isola was in very high spirits, and her husband was delighted at the change from that growing apathy which had so frightened him. The ladies had scarcely left the table when Captain Hulbert arrived, and was ushered into the dining-room, where Martin Disney was smoking his after-dinner pipe in the chimney corner— the old chimney corner of that original Angler's Nest, which had been a humble homestead two hundred years ago.

The two men shook hands, and then John Hulbert seated himself on the opposite side of the hearth, and they began to talk earnestly of the future, Martin Disney speaking with fond affection of the sister who had been to him almost as a daughter.

"Her mother was the sweetest and truest of women," he said, "and her father had one of the most refined and delicate natures I ever met with in a man. I do not know that he was altogether fitted for the Church. He was wanting in energy and decision, or force of character; but he was a firm believer, pure-minded and disinterested, and he was an artist to the tips of his fingers. It is from him

Allegra inherits her love of art; only while he was content to trifle with art she has worked with all the power of her strong, resolute temperament. She inherits that from her mother's line, which was a race of workers, men with whom achievement was a necessity of existence—men who fought, and men who thought—sword and gown."

Disney smiled at the stern condition of a year's probation which Allegra had imposed upon her lover.

"Such sentences are very often remitted," he said.

"I own to having some hope of mercy," replied Captain Hulbert. "People have an idea that May marriages are unlucky; and perhaps we had better defer to a popular superstition. But it seems to me that June is a capital month for a yachtsman's honeymoon; and if I can persuade my dearest to remit half my period of probation, and fix the 1st of June for our wedding, I should be just half a year happier than I am now."

"Have you any notion yet what kind of life you are to lead after your marriage? I hope it will not be a roving life. Isola and I would like to have our sister near us."

"And Allegra and I would like to study your liking," laughed Hulbert. "We may wander a little on summer seas, but we will have our fixed abode, and it shall be near you. So long as Lostwithiel is a bachelor, we can make our home at the Mount; but fond as I am of that dear old place, I should be glad to see my brother married. There is something amiss in his present mode of life; and I have but too strong reason to fear that he is not a happy man."

"Have you any idea of the cause of his un-happiness?"

"Only speculative ideas—mere theories that may be without foundation in fact. I fancy that he has burnt the lamp of life a little too furiously, and that the light has grown dim in the socket. The after-taste of a fiery youth is the taste of dust and ashes. There may be memories, too—memories of some past folly— which are vivid enough to poison the present. I know that he is unhappy. I have tried to find out the cause; and it all ends in this—an obstinate reserve on his part, and mere theorizing on mine."

"I have heard that he lived in a bad set after he left the University?"

"A bad set—yes, that is it. A man who begins life in a certain circle is like a workman who gets his arm or his leg caught unawares in a machine worked by steam power. In an instant he is entangled past rescue. He is gone. A man takes the wrong road. Ten years afterwards, perhaps, when he is bald and wrinkled, he may pull himself up on the downward track and try to get rid of a bad reputation and make a fresh start; but those fresh starts rarely end in a winning race. I am very sorry for my brother. He is a warm-hearted fellow, with a good deal of talent; and he ought not to have made a bad thing of his life."

"Let us hope that he has pulled up in time, and that he may get a young wife before he is many years older. I have no desire that my sister's son should be a peer. I only want to see her happy with a husband who shall be worthy of her."

CHAPTER VI.

"I HAVE YOU STILL, THE SUN COMES OUT AGAIN."

THE new year was just a week old, and Isola and Allegra were standing on a terraced hillside in a country where January has noontides as brilliant and balmy as an English June. They had travelled up that almost perpendicular hill in a roomy landau drawn by a pair of horses, and now, near the summit of the hill, on the last of those many terraces that zig-zag up the face of the cliff, they had alighted from the carriage, and were standing side by side upon the broad white road, at an angle where the cliff dipped suddenly, clothed with the wild growth of stunted olive and bushy pine, down and down to the abyss where the blue sea looked like a sapphire at the bottom of a pit. They stood and gazed, and gazed again, almost bewildered by the infinite beauty and variety of that dazzling prospect.

Below them, in the shelter of the land-locked bay, Ospedaletti's pavilioned Casino shone whitely out of a garden of palm and cactus, with terrace and balustrade vanishing down to the sea. To the left, the steep promontory of Bordighera jutted far out into the blue; and over the rugged crest of the hill Mentone's long white line lay in a gentle curve, almost level with the sea—a strip of vivid white between the blue of the water and the gloom of that great barren mountain wall which marks the beginning of modern Italy. And beyond, again, showed the twin towers of Monaco; and further still, in the dim blue distance, one saw the battlemented line of the Esterelles, dividing the fairyland of the Riviera from the workaday prose of shipbuilding Toulon and commercial Marseilles.

On this side of those pine-clad mountains there were only pleasure and fancy, wealth, fashion, the languid invalid, and the feverish gambler; on the other side there were toilers and speculators, the bourse and the factory, the world of stern realities.

To the right, deep down within the hills, lay the little port of San Remo, with its rugged stone pier and its shabby old houses, and the old, old town climbing up the steep ascent to that isolated point where the white dome of the Sanctuary shone out against the milky azure of the noontide sky; and further and further away stretched the long line of the olive-clothed hills, to the purple distance, where the seamen's church of Madonna della Guardia stands boldly out between sky and sea, as if it were a half-way house on the upward road to heaven.

"How lovely it all is!" cried Allegra. "But don't you feel that one careless step upon that flowery edge yonder would send us whirling down the cliffs to awful, inevitable death? When that man passed us just now with his loaded cart, I felt sick with fear—the wheels seemed to graze the edge of the abyss as the horse crept slowly along—poor stolid brute!— unconscious of his danger. It is a dreadful drive, Isola, this zigzag road to Colla—slant above slant, backwards and forwards, up the face of this prodigious cliff. I had to shut my eyes at every turn of the road, when the world below seemed to swim in a chaos of light and colour—so beautiful, so terrible! Do you see the height of those cliffs, terrace above terrace, hill above hill? Why, that level road at the very bottom is the top of a taller cliff than those I used to think so appalling at Broadstairs and Ramsgate!"

"I don't think it would make much difference to a man who fell over the edge whether he fell here or in the Isle of Thanet," said Martin Disney, as he stood, with his arm drawn through his wife's, sweeping the prospect with his field glass.

"Oh, but it would! One would be only a sudden shock and a plunge into the sea, or swift annihilation on the rocks below; but from this awful height, to go whirling down, plucked at here by an olive branch, or there by a jagged rock, yet always whirling downward, rebounding from edge to edge, faster, and faster, and faster, till one were dashed into a shapeless mass on that white road yonder!"

"And to think of people living up there in the clouds, and going to sleep every night with the knowledge of this mighty wall and that dreadful abyss in their minds!" she concluded, pointing upward to where the little white town of Colla straggled along the edge of the hill.

They were going up to see the pictures and books in the little museum by the church. It was their first excursion, since their arrival in Italy, for Martin Disney had been anxious that his wife should be thoroughly rested after her long journey, before she was called upon to make the slightest exertion. She was looking better and stronger already, they were both agreed; and she was looking happier, a fact which gave her husband infinite satisfaction. They had come by the St. Gothard, taking their ease as they came along the familiar route, the way they had travelled on their road to Venice and the East. They had rested a night at Dover and a night at Basle, and had stopped at Lucerne for three days, and again a couple of days at Milan, and again at Genoa, exploring the city, and the Campo Santo in a leisurely way; Allegra exalted out of herself almost by the delight of those wonderful collections in the palaces of the Via Balbi—the Veroneses, the Titians, the

Guidos—Isola languidly admiring, languidly wondering at everything, but only deeply moved when they came to the strange city of the dead, the scenic representation of sickness, calamity, grief and dissolution, in every variety of realistic representation or of classic emblem. Sculptured scenes of domestic sorrow, dying fathers, kneeling children, weeping widows —whole families convulsed in the throes of that last inevitable parting; the death of youth and beauty; the fallen rose-wreath; the funeral urn; the lowered torch; and the ball-dress; hyacinth and butterfly; Psyche and Apollo; the fatal river and the fatal boat; grimness and beauty—the actual and the allegorical curiously mixed in the sculptured images that line the cold white colonades, where the footsteps of holiday-makers echo with a sepulchral sound under the vaulted roof. Here Isola was intensely interested, and insisted on going up the marble steps, flight after flight, and to the very summit of the hill of graves, with its wide-reaching prospect of mountain, and fort, and city, and sea.

"Think how hard it must be to lie here and know nothing of all that loveliness," she said, her

eyes widening with wonder as they gazed across
the varied perspective of vale and mountain, out
to the faint blue sea. "How hard, how hard!
Do they feel it and know it, Allegra? Can this
I—which feels so keenly, which only sleeps in
order to enter a new world of dreams—busier
and more crowded and more eventful than the
real world—can this consciousness go out all at
once like the flame of a candle—and nothing,
nothing, nothing be left?"

"They are not here," said Allegra, with gentle
seriousness. "It is only the husk that lies here
—the flower-seed has been carried off in God's
great wind of death—and the flower is blossom-
ing somewhere else."

"One allegory is as good as another," said
Isola. "We can but console ourselves with
symbols. I don't like this crowded city of the
dead, Allegra. For God's sake, don't let Martin
have me buried here, if I should die at San
Remo!"

"Dearest, why will you harbour such ghastly
thoughts?"

"Oh, it was only a passing fancy. I thought
it just possible that if I were to die while we

are in Italy, Martin might think to honour me by having me laid in this splendid cemetery. He seemed so struck by the grandeur and beauty of the monuments, just now, when we were in those colonades down yonder."

Colonel Disncy had lingered a little way off to look at Mazzini's monument. He came up to them now, and hurried them back to the gate, where their carriage was waiting. And so ended their last afternoon in Genoa; and the most vivid picture of the city and its surroundings that Isola carried away with her was the picture of those marble tombs upon the hill, and those tall and gloomy cypresses which are the trees of death.

Yes, she was better, gayer, and more active—more like the girl-wife whom Martin Disney had carried home to Cornwall, prouder than Tristan when he sailed away with Irish Iseult.

The Italian sunshine had revived his fading flower, Disney told himself, ready to love all things in a land that had brought the smiles back to his wife's pale lips, and a new and delicate bloom to her wan cheeks. Yes, she was happier than she had been of late in Cornwall; there could be no doubt as to that.

They stayed at a hotel for more than a week, while they deliberated upon the choice of a villa. They found one at last, which seemed to realize their ideas of perfection. It was not a grand or stately dwelling. No marble bell-tower or architectural loggia attracted the eye of the passing pedestrian. It was roomy, and bright, and clean, and airy, built rather in the Swiss than the Italian style, and it stood upon the slope of the hill on the west side of the town, with nothing but olive-woods between its terraced garden and the road that skirted the sea. It was a reminiscence of the Alps, built by a retired merchant of Zurich, and its owner had called it Lauter Brunnen. The house was at most two years old; but life's vicissitudes had left it empty for a year and a half, and the rent asked of Colonel Disney was much less than he had been prepared to pay.

The installation was full of delight for Isola and her sister-in-law. The house afforded innumerable surprises, unexpected nooks and corners of all kinds. There were lovely views from every window—east, west, north, or south—and there was a garden full of roses, a garden made upon so steep a slope that it was a succession of terraces, with but little intervening level ground, and below the lowest terrace the valley stretched down to the sea, a tangle of gnarled old olive trees, wan and silvery, with a ruined gateway just seen among the foliage at the bottom of a dim grey glade.

To the right, straggling along the edge of the wooded hill, appeared the white houses and churches, cupola, pinnacle, and dome of Colla, so scattered as to seem two towns rather than one, and with picturesque suggestions of architectural splendour that were hardly borne out by the reality, when one climbed those rugged mule-paths, and crossed the romantic gorge above the waterfall, and then upward and upward to the narrow alleys and crumbling archways, and the spacious old church with its lofty doorway standing high above the stony street.

Only a few paces from Colonel Disney's villa there was a stately house that had gone to ruin. The roof was off in some places; there were neither floors nor windows left; and the walls were open to the wind and rain—frescoed walls, upon which might be traced figures of saint and martyr, angel and madonna. There was a spacious garden, with an avenue of cypresses—a garden where the flowers had been growing wild for years, and where Isola and Allegra wandered and explored as they pleased. It was higher on the hillside than their own villa, and from the eastward edge of this garden they looked—across a yawning gulf in which lay all the lower town of San Remo—to the Sanctuary and the Leper Hospital, conspicuous on the crest of the opposite hill.

The need for Citadel and Sanctuary had passed with the fiercer age in which they were built. Neither Saracen nor pirate menaced San Remo nowadays; but the old white walls made a picturesque note in the landscape, and the very name of Sanctuary had a romantic sound.

The first week in the new house was like a week in fairyland. The weather was peerless— a climate that makes people forget there is such a season as winter in the world—and the two girls wandered about in the olive woods and climbed

the mule-paths all through the fresh balmy hours;
or in the hottest noontides sat in the deserted
garden or in a sheltered corner near an old stone
well—one of those wells which suggest the
meeting of Isaac and Rebecca—and Allegra
painted while Isola read to her, in the low sweet
voice which lent new and individual music to the
sweetest verse of her favourites, Byron, Keats,
and Shelley.

In these sequestered spots, where only a peasant woman laden with a basket of olives, or a
padre, going from Colla to San Remo, ever passed
within sight of them, they read the Eve of St.
Agnes and the Pot of Basil—the Prisoner of
Chillon, Manfred, and all those familiar lyrics
and favourite passages of Shelley which Isola
held in her heart of hearts. The wonder-dream
of Alastor—the passionate lament of Adonaïs,
could not seem purer or more spiritual than
the life of these young women in those calm
days through which January slipped into
February, unawares, like a link in a golden
chain—a chain of sunshine and flowers.

In February came the Carnival; and pretty
little rustic San Remo decked itself with bunting

and greenery, and made believe to hold a Battle
of Flowers, which had a certain village simplicity
as compared with the serried ranks of carriages,
the fashion, and beauty, and wealth of floral
displays, along the Promenade des Anglais or the
Croisette.   With the Carnival came the mistral,
which generally seems to be waiting round the
corner ready to leap out upon the flower-throwers,
to blight their bouquets, and blow dust into the
eyes of beauty, and make the feeble health-
seekers cower in the corners of their rose-decked
carriages.   This Lenten season was no exception
to other seasons; and the calendar—which had
been as it were in abeyance since New Year's Day
—came into force again—and stern and sterile
Winter said, "Here am I. Did you think I
had forgotten you?" The invalids were roughly
awakened from their dream of Paradise, to
discover that February even in San Remo meant
February, and could not always be mistaken for
May or June.

Isola felt the change, though she was hardly
conscious of it on the day of the floral battle,
when she was sitting in a roomy landau, covered
with the dark shining foliage and pale yellow

fruit from some of those lemon trees in the orchard where she and Allegra had spent their morning hours. Allegra had planned the decorations, and had gone down to the coach-house to assist in the work, delighted to chatter with the coachman in doubtful Italian, groping her way in a language in which her whole stock-in-trade consisted of a few quotations from Dante or Petrarch—and all the wise saws of Dr. Riccabocca.

"I would have none of that horrid pepper tree which pervades the place with its floppy foliage, and dull red fruit," she told Isola, descanting on the result of her exertions. "I was rather taken with the pepper trees at first, but I am satiated with their languid grace. They are like the weeping ash or the weeping willow. There is no real grace or beauty in them. I would rather have one of those cypresses towering up among the grey-green olives in the valley below Colla than all the pepper trees in the public gardens. I have used no flowers but narcissus; no colour but the pale gold of the lemons and the dark green of the leaves; except one bit of audacity which you will see presently."

This was at noon, after two hours' work in the coach-house. An hour later the carriage was at the door.

Allegra's audacity was an Algerian curtain, a rainbow of vivid colour, with which she had draped the back of the landau, hiding all the ugliness of rusty leather. The carriage, or it might have been the two girlish faces in it, one so pale and gentle, the other so brilliant and changeful in its lights and shadows, made the point of attraction in the little procession. Everybody spoke of the two girls in the lemon landau, with the nice-looking, middle-aged man. Were they his daughters, people wondered, or his nieces ; and at what hotel were they staying ? It was a disappointment to discover that they were living in that villa to the west of the town, out of the way of everything and everybody, and that they were seldom to be seen in public, except at the new church, where they were regular worshippers.

"The man is Colonel Disney, and the tall, striking-looking girl is his wife," said one person better informed than the rest, but making a wrong selection all the same.

CHAPTER VII.

"THOU PARADISE OF EXILES, ITALY."

ISOLA was not quite so well after that drive in the February wind and dust. She developed a slight cough—very slight and inoffensive; but still it was a cough—and the kind and clever physician of San Remo, who came to see her once a week or so, told her to be careful. Mr. Baynham had written him a long letter about his patient, and the San Remo doctor felt a friendly interest in Isola and her sister-in-law, and the baby son in whom the whole family were so intensely interested. The infant had accepted the change in his surroundings with supreme complaisance, and crowed and chirruped among the lemons and the olives, and basked in the Southern sunshine, as his nurse wheeled his perambulator to and fro upon the terraced road behind the villa—the road which lost itself a little way further on amidst a wilderness of olives, and dwindled into a narrow track for man or mule.

The flower-battle was over, and the mistral had gone back to the great wind-cavern to lie in wait for the next golden opportunity; and the sun was shining once again upon the hills where the oil mills nestled, clinging to some rough ledge beside the ever-dropping waters, upon the labyrinthine lanes and alleys, the queer little flights of stone steps up which a figure like Ali Baba might generally be seen leading his heavily-laden, long-suffering donkey; upon arch and cupola, church and market-place, and on the triple rampart of hills that shuts San Remo from the outer world. The Disneys had been in Italy nearly seven weeks, and it seemed as natural to Isola to open her eyes upon the broad blue waters of the Mediterranean, the gorgeous sunrise, and the lateen sails, as on the Fowey river and the hills towards Polruan. She had taken kindly to this Italian exile. The sun and the blue sky had exercised a healing influence upon that hidden wound which had once made her heart seem one dull, aching pain. She loved this new world of wood and hill, and most of all she loved the perfect liberty of this distant retreat, and the consolations of solitude. As for the cough, or the pain in her side, or any of those other symptoms about which the doctor talked to her so gravely, she made very light of them. She was happy in her husband's love, happy in his society, strolling with him in the olive wood, or the deserted garden, or down to the little toy-shop parade by the sea, where the band played once a week ; or to the other garden in the town, where the same band performed on another day, and which was dustier and less airy than the little plantation of palm and cactus upon the edge of the sea. She went for excursions with him to points of especial beauty high up among the hills—to the chocolate mill, to San Romolo, she riding a donkey, he at the animal's side, while the guide trudged cheerily in the dust at the edge of the mountain road. In the evening she played to him, or sat by his side while he smoked the pipe of rest, or worked while he read to her. They had never been more devoted to each other, never more like wedded lovers than they were now. People who only knew them by sight talked of them admiringly, as if their love were an interesting phenomenon.

"He must be twenty years older than his wife," said Society, "and yet they seem so happy together. It is quite refreshing to see such a devoted couple nowadays."

People always seem ready and rather pleased to hold their own age up to contempt and ridicule, as if they themselves did not belong to it; as if they were sitting aloft in a balloon, looking down at the foolish creatures crawling and crowding upon the earth, in a spirit of philosophical contemplation.

One only anxiety troubled Isola at this time, and that was on Allegra's account rather than her own. They had left England nearly two months, and as yet there had been no sign or token of any kind from Captain Hulbert, not so much as a packet of new books or new music— not so much as a magazine or an illustrated paper.

"He asked if he might write to me, and I told him no," Allegra said, rather dolefully, one morning, as they sat a little way from the well, Allegra engaged in painting a brown-skinned peasant girl of ten years old, whom she had met carrying olives the night before, and had forthwith engaged as a model. " I said it would never do for us to begin the folly of engaged lovers, who write to each other about nothing, sometimes twice a day. He has been wonderfully obedient: yet I think he ought to have written once or twice in two months. He ought to have known that though I told him not to write, I should be very anxious to hear from him."

"You mustn't be surprised at his obeying you to the letter, Allegra. There is a kind of simplicity about him, although he is very clever. He is so thoroughly frank and honest. It is for that I honour him."

"Yes, he is very good," sighed Allegra. "I ought not to have told him I would have no letter-writing. I really meant what I said. I wanted to give myself up to art, and you, for the unbroken year—to have no other thought, no distractions—and I knew that his letters would be a distraction—that the mere expectation of them—the looking for post time—the wondering whether I should have his letter by this or that post—I knew all that kind of thing would unnerve me. My hand would have lost its power. You don't know what it is when all depends upon certainty of touch—the fine obedience of the hand to the eye. No, his letters would have been a daily agitation—and yet, and yet I should like so much to know what he is doing—if he is still at the Mount— if he has any idea of coming to San Remo later —with his yacht—as he talked of doing."

"I have no doubt he will come. It will be the most natural thing for him to do. You will see the white sails some afternoon, glorified in the sunset, like that boat yonder with its amethyst-coloured sail."

Isola was right in her prophecy, except as to the hour of Captain Hulbert's arrival. They were taking a picnic luncheon in a little grove of lemon and orange, wedged into a cleft in the hills, on the edge of a deep and narrow gorge down which a mountain torrent rushed to the sea. Suddenly across the narrow strip of blue at the end of the vista came the vision of white sails, a schooner with all her canvas spread, dazzling in the noonday sun, sailing towards San Remo. Allegra sat gazing at the white sails, but said never a word. Neither Martin Disney nor his wife happened to be looking that way, till the child in his nurse's lap gave a sudden crow of delight.

"Did he see the pretty white ship, then?" said the nurse, holding him up in the sunshine. "The beautiful white ship."

No one took any notice. The colonel was reading his *Times*, the chief link between the exile and civilization. Isola was intent upon knitting a soft white wool vestment for her firstborn.

Two hours later the garden gate gave a little click, and Captain Hulbert walked in. Allegra heard the click of the latch as she sat in the verandah, and ran out to meet him. She had been watching and expectant all the time, though she had held her peace about the vision of white sails, lest she should be suspected of hoping for her lover's coming, and, above all, lest she should be compassionated with later in the day, if the ship were not the *Vendetta*.

Yes, it was he. She turned pale with delight at the realization of her hope. She had hardly known till this instant how much she loved him. She let him take her in his arms and kiss her, just as if he had been the commonest sailor whose " heart was true to Poll."

"Are you really glad to see me, darling ? " he whispered, overcome by the delight of this fond welcome.

"Really glad. I feel as if we had been parted for years. No letter to tell me where you were or what you were doing ! I began to doubt if you ever cared for me."

" Heartless infidel, you told me not to write ; and so I thought the only alternative was to come. And I have been coming for the last five weeks. We had a stiffish time across the bay, and my auxiliary engine went wrong— nothing to trust to but canvas ; so I had to waste a week at Toulon while my ship was under repairs. However, here I am, and the *Vendetta* is safe and sound ; and I am your most obedient slave. How is Mrs. Disney ? "

" Not quite so well as she was two or three weeks ago. She improved wonderfully at first, but she caught cold one bleak, blowy day, and she has started a little nervous kind of cough, which makes us anxious about her."

"Better spirits, I hope. Not quite so mopy?"

"Her spirits have revived wonderfully. This lovely land has given her a new life. But there are times when she droops a little. She is curiously sensitive—too impressionable for happiness. We have a very fine preacher here—Father Rodwell; you must have heard him."

"Yes, I heard of him at Oxford. He was before my time by some years; but he was a celebrity, and I heard men talk of him. Well, what of your preacher? Has he fallen in love with my Allegra—is he in the same boat as poor Colfox?"

"Fallen in love! No, he is not that kind of man. He is as earnest and enthusiastic as a mediæval monk. We have all been carried away by his eloquence. He preaches what people call awakening sermons; and I fear they have been too agitating for Isola. She insists on hearing him; she hangs upon his words; but his preaching has too strong an influence upon her mind—or upon her nerves. I have seen the tears streaming down her poor pale cheeks; I have seen her terribly overcome. She is too weak to bear that kind of strain. She is depressed all the rest of the day."

"She ought not to be allowed to hear such sermons. Take her to another church, where some dosy old bird will send her comfortably to sleep."

"I have tried to take her to the other church—you must not talk of a clergyman as a dosy old bird, sir—but she looked so unhappy at the mere idea of missing Father Rodwell's sermons that I dare not press the matter. He comes to see us occasionally, and he is the cheeriest and pleasantest of men, nothing of the zealot or ascetic about him; so that I am in hopes his influence will be for good in the long run. How long shall you be able to stop at San Remo?"

"Till the lady for whose sake I came shall take it into her head to leave the place. I have been thinking, Allegra," putting his arm through hers, and pacing up and down the terrace, with the bright expanse of sea in front of them, and at their back the great curtain of hills encircling and defending them from the northern world—

"I have been thinking that Venice would be a charming place for you and me to spend next summer in—if—if—you meant six months instead of twelve for my probation—as I really think you must have done. We could be married on the first of June—such a pretty date for a wedding! You would want to be married in Trelasco Church, of course; on our native soil. The church in which my great-grandfather was married, and in which I and all my race were christened! We could have the yacht at Marseilles ready to carry us off to the south, through the delicious summer days and nights, all along this lovely coast, and away by Naples to the Adriatic. Allegra, why should we wait for the winter, the dreary winter, to begin our life journey? Let us begin it in the time of roses."

"Look, George!" cried Allegra, laughing, as she pointed to the hedge of red roses in front of them, and the clusters of creamy bloom hanging over the verandah. "The roses have been blooming ever since we came to Italy. It is always rose-time here. You remember our reading in the dedication of 'To Leeward' how Marion

Crawford strewed his wife's pathway with roses on Christmas Day at Sorrento. We can find a flowery land for our honeymoon at any season of the year."

"But why wait a year? Can you not prove me trusty and true in less than a year?"

"You are so impatient," she said, plucking a handful of roses, and scattering the petals at her feet. "A year is so short a time."

"Short, love! why, eight weeks have seemed an eternity to me without you; and you honoured me just now by saying that the time had appeared long, even to you—even to my liege lady, sitting serene in her palace of art, painting contadinas and their olive-faced offspring—even to you, whose love is as a thread of silk against a cable, compared to mine. Even to you, my mistress and my tyrant."

"That was because you were so far away. But there will be nothing to hinder our seeing each other, as often as you may find convenient. I have set my heart upon painting steadily for a twelvemonth, without any distractions."

"There is no such place as Venice for a painter. Think of the Miss Montalbas, and the splendid work they have done at Venice. Would you not like to be like them?"

"Would I not like to be like Apelles?"

"Well, Venice will be your treasury; Venice will fill that busy brain with ideas. You shall be fed upon pictures old and new—the new living pictures in the narrow streets and canals; the old masters in the churches and palaces. You shall learn of Tintoret and Veronese. You shall paint as much as you like. You shall have no distractions. We shall be strangers there, can live as we choose. Summer is the time for Venice, Allegra. Benighted English people have an idea that Italy is a place to winter in, and they go and shiver in marble palaces, and watch the torrential rain beating against windows that were never meant to shut out bad weather. The Italians know that their land is a land of summer, and they know how to enjoy sunny days and balmy nights. You don't know how delicious life is on the Lido when the night is only a brief interval of starshine betwixt sunset and dawn. You don't know what a dream of delight it is to float along the lagoons and watch the lamp-lit city melt into the mists of evening, breathing faint echoes of music and song. A great many things of beauty have been turned to ugliness, Allegra, since printing and the steam engine were invented; but, thank God! Venice is not one of them. You will think of my plan, won't you, love? At the least, it is a thing to be considered."

"Anything you say is worthy to be considered, John. And now come in and see Isola and Martin."

He felt that he had gone far enough—he felt that it were unwise to press the question too much at first. He meant to be gently persistent; and he meant to have his own way.

He followed Allegra into the drawing-room—a room full of light and sunshine, which had been beautified and made homelike by the addition of a few Japaneseries and a little old Italian furniture which Martin Disney had picked up at a bric-à-brac shop in the Via Vittorio Emanuelo. There were flowers everywhere, in the bright Italian pottery, with its varieties of form and colouring. To Hulbert's fancy it was the prettiest room he had seen for an age.

"You seem to have made yourself uncommonly

comfortable here," he said, after cordial greetings, settling down into a bamboo chair near Isola's little olive-wood table, with its litter of Tauchnitz novels and fancy work. "It is a pleasant sensation for a rolling stone who has hardly ever known what home means to drop into such a nest as this. You will have too much of my company, I'm afraid. You'll be shocked to hear that I have taken rooms at the Anglais, down there," pointing down the valley, " within a stone's throw of you."

"We are not shocked. We are very glad you will be near us," said Isola, smiling at him. "It has been a dull life for Allegra, I'm afraid."

"Dull! dull in this land of beauty!" cried Allegra. "I have never known a dull hour since I came here; though, of course," with a shy glance at her lover, "I have naturally thought sometimes of absent friends, and wished they were with me to revel in the loveliness of these woods and hills."

" Well, one of your friends has come to you, one who would as gladly have come had you been in regions where the sun never shines, or where his chariot wheels scorch the torrid sands."

Captain Hulbert stayed with them all the evening, and planned a sail to Mentone for the following day, Isola again begging to be left out of their plans, as she had done at Fowey.

"You need feel no compunction about leaving me," she said. "I shall be perfectly happy in the woods with nurse, and baby, and my books."

They obeyed her, and the little excursion was arranged. They were to start soon after the early breakfast, carrying what their Italian butler called a pique-nique with them, in the shape of a well-provided luncheon-basket. Isola sat in the olive wood, watching the white sails moving slowly towards Bordighera. It was an exquisite day, but with scarcely a puff of wind; a day for dreaming on the water rather than for rapid progress. The yacht scarcely seemed to move as Isola watched her from the cushioned corner which Löttchen had arranged in an angle of the low stone wall—all amongst ferns and mosses, brown orchises and blue violets—an angle sheltered by a century-old olive, whose gnarled trunk sprawled along the ground, rugged and riven, but with another century's life in it yet. Far down in the valley, below the old gateway, a company of cypresses rose dark against the blue of the sea, and Isola knew that just on that slope of the shore where the cypresses grew tallest the graves of English exiles were gathered. Many a fair hope, many a broken dream, many a disappointed ambition lay at rest under those dark spires, within the sound of that summer sea.

This was one of many days which the young mother spent in the woods or in the garden with her baby for her companion, while Allegra and the colonel sailed east or west in the *Vendetta*. Her doctor would have liked her to go with them, but she seemed to have an absolute aversion to the sea, and he did not press the point.

"Nothing that she dislikes will do her any good," he told Colonel Disney. "There is no use in being persistent about anything. Fancies and whims stand for a great deal in such an illness as hers."

A week or two later the same kind doctor discovered that his patient was fast losing ground. Her strength had flagged considerably in a short time. He recommended change of scene.

"This quiet life suited her wonderfully well

for the first month or so, but we are no longer making any headway. You had better try a gayer place—a little more life and movement."

Martin Disney was ready to obey. He and Allegra took counsel together, and then—in the lightest strain, one evening after dinner—they discussed the notion of a change.

"Shall we strike our tents, Isola? Are you tired of San Remo?"

"No, Martin. I am tired of myself, sometimes —never of these olive woods and lemon groves. Sometimes the stillness and the silent beauty of the place make me feel unhappy, without knowing why; but that is a kind of unhappiness no one can escape."

"Is there any place in the world within tolerably easy reach of this that you would like to see?" asked her husband.

"Yes, there is one city in the world that I have been longing to see ever since I began to have thoughts and wishes."

"And that is—— "

"Rome! I should like to see Rome before I die, Martin; if it were not too troublesome for you—— "

"Troublesome! My dearest, can anything be troublesome to me if it can but give you pleasure? You shall see Rome—not once—but again and again, in the course of a long and happy life, I hope. I am nearly thirty years older than you; but I count upon at least thirty years more upon this planet, before I blow out my candle and say ' *Bon soir.*' "

"God grant that you may live to a good old age, Martin. The world is better for such a man as you."

"The world would be no place for me without my wife," he said. "And so you would like to see Rome, Isa? What has put that fancy into your head?"

"Oh, it is an old dream, as I said just now. And lately I have been talking to Father Rodwell, who knows Rome as well as if he were a Roman citizen, and he has made me more and more anxious to go there. If it would not be a great plague to you, Martin."

"On the contrary, it would be a great pleasure. We will go to Rome, Isa, if your doctor approve. Allegra will like it, I know."

"Like it?" echoed Allegra, "I shall simply

be intoxicated with delight. I know the catalogues of all the picture-galleries by heart. I think I know every one of the seven hills as well as if I had walked upon them from my childhood. I have read so many descriptions of the place and its surroundings—so many raptures penned by people whom I have envied for nothing else than that. They have known Rome; they have lived in Rome."

The whole business was easily settled. Captain Hulbert was the only person who regretted the change. He had been a month at San Remo, a month of summer idleness in February and March, a month of summer sails on an azure sea; of mountain walks and rides, high up from stage to stage, until the region of lemon groves and olive woods gave place to the pines on the loftier hills. He had been able to spend all his days in Allegra's society.

There were no pictures, except in that one little gallery at Colla. There was nothing to distract her from her lover. In Rome there would be all the wonders of the most wonderful city in the world. It would be art first and love second.

The doctor approved; Father Rodwell wrote to an agent in Rome, and after some negotiation a suite of apartments was found on the high ground near the Trinità de' Monte, which seemed to meet all the requirements of the case. The priest vouched for the honesty and good faith of the agent, and on his responsibility the rooms were taken for the month of April, with liberty to occupy them later if it were so desired.

CHAPTER VIII

"THE WOODS ARE ROUND US, HEAPED AND DIM."

IT was their last day at San Remo. Everything
had been packed for the journey, and the drawing-room at Lauter Brunnen had a dreary look
now that it was stripped of all those decorations
and useful prettinesses with which Allegra had
made it so gay and home-like.

The morning was brilliant, and Martin, Allegra,
and Captain Hulbert set off at nine o'clock upon
a long-deferred expedition to San Romolo. They
would be home in good time for the eight-o'clock
dinner; and Isola promised to amuse herself all
day, and to be in good spirits to welcome them
on their return.

"You have a duty to do for your sister," she
said, when her husband felt compunction at

leaving her. "Think of all she has done for us, her devotion, her unselfishness. The least we can do is to help her to be happy with her lover; and all the burden of that duty has fallen upon you. I think you ought to be called Colonel Gooseberry."

She looked a bright and happy creature as she stood on the mule-path in the olive wood, waving her hand to them as they went away—Allegra riding a donkey, the two men walking, one on each side of her bridle, and the driver striding on ahead, leading a riderless donkey which was to serve as an occasional help by-and-by, if either of the pedestrians wanted a lift. Her cheeks were flushed with walking, and her eyes were bright with a new gladness.

She was full of a childish pleasure in the idea of their journey, and the realization of a dream which most of us have dreamt a long time before it assumed the shape of earthly things—the dream of Rome.

Isola stood listening to their footsteps, as they passed the little painted shrine on the hill path She heard them give the time of day to a party of peasant women, with empty baskets on their heads, going up to gather the last of the olives. Then she roamed about the wooded valley and the slope of the hill towards Colla for over an hour, and then, growing suddenly tired, she crept home, in time to sit beside her baby while he slept his placid noontide sleep. She bent over the little rosebud mouth and kissed it, in a rapture of maternal love.

"So young to see Rome," she murmured, " and to think that those star-like eyes will see and take no heed ; to think that such a glorious vision will pass before him, and yet he will remember nothing."

The day was very long, something like one of those endless days at Trelasco, when her husband was in Burmah and she had only the dog and the cat for her companions. She thought of those fond friends to-day with a regretful sigh—the sleepy Shah, so calm and undemonstrative in his attachment, but with a placid, purring delight in her society which seemed to mean a great deal ; the fox-terrier, so active and intense in his affection, demanding so much attention, intruding himself upon her walks and reveries with such eager, not-to-be-denied

devotion. She had no four-footed friends here;
and the want of them made an empty space in
her life.

In the afternoon the weather changed suddenly.
The sky became overcast, the sea a leaden colour;
and the mistral came whistling up the valley
with a great rustling and shivering of the silver-
green foliage and creaking of the old bent
branches, like the withered arms of witch or
sorceress. All the glory of the day was gone,
and the white villas on the crest of the eastward
hill stood out with a livid distinctness against the
blackened sky.

Isola wandered up the hill-path, past the little
shrine where the way divided, the point at which
she had seen her husband and his party vanish
in the sunny morning. She felt a sudden sense
of loneliness now the sun was gone; a childish
longing for the return of her friends, for evening
and lamplight, and the things that make for
cheerfulness. She was cold and dull, and out
of spirits. She had left the house while the sun
was shining, and she had come without shawl or
wrap of any kind, and the mistral made her
shiver. Yet she had no idea of hurrying home.

The loneliness of the house had become oppressive before she left it; and she knew there would be some hours to wait for the return of the excursionists. So she mounted the steep mule-path, slowly and painfully, till she had gone two-thirds of the way to Colla; and then she sat down to rest on the low stone wall which enclosed a little garden in a break of the wood, from which point there was a far-stretching view seaward.

She was very cold, but she was so tired as to be glad to rest at any hazard of after-suffering. Drowsy from sheer exhaustion, she leant her head against a great rugged olive, whose roots were mixed up with the wall, and fell fast asleep. She awoke, shivering, from a confused dream of sea and woods, Roman temples and ruined palaces. She had been wandering in one of those dream-cities that have neither limit nor settled locality. It was here in the woods below Colla, and yet was half Rome and half Trelasco. There was a classic temple upon a hill that was like the Mount, and the day was bleak, and dark, and rainy, and she was walking on the footpath through Lord Lostwithiel's park, with

the storm-driven rain beating against her face,
just as on that autumn evening, when the owner
of the soil had taken compassion upon her and
had given her shelter. The dream had been
curiously vivid—a dream which brought the past
back as if it were the present, and blotted out all
that had come afterwards. She woke bewildered,
forgetting that her husband had come back from
India, and that she was in Italy, thinking of
herself as she had been that October evening
when she and Lostwithiel met for the first time.

The sea was darker than when she fell asleep.
There was the dull crimson of a stormy sunset
yonder, behind the jutting promontory of Bordighera, while the sky above was barred with long,
black clouds, and the wind was howling across
the great deep valley like an evil spirit tortured
and imprisoned, shrieking to his gods for release.
Exactly opposite her, as she stood in the deep
cleft of the hills, a solitary vessel was labouring
under press of canvas towards the point upon
whose dusky summit the chapel of the Madonna
della Guardia gleamed whitely in the dying day.
The vessel was a schooner yacht, of considerable
tonnage, certainly larger than the *Vendetta*.

Isola stood, still as marble, watching that labouring boat, the straining sails, the dark hull beaten by the stormy dash of the waves. She watched with wide, open eyes, and parted lips, quivering as with an over-mastering fear, watched in momentary expectation of seeing those straining sails dip for the last time, that labouring hull capsize and vanish betwixt black wave and white surf. She watched in motionless attention till the boat disappeared behind the shoulder of the hill; and then, shivering, nervous, and altogether over-strung, she hurried homewards, feeling that she had stayed out much too long, and that she had caught a chill which might be the cause of new trouble.

If those narrow mule-paths had been less familiar, she might have lost her way in the dusk; but she had trodden them too often to be in any difficulty, and she reached the villa without loss of time, but not before the return of the picnic party.

Allegra and Captain Hulbert were at the gate watching for her. Colonel Disney had gone into the wood to look for her, and had naturally taken the wrong direction.

"Oh, Isola; how could you stop out so late, and on such a stormy evening?" remonstrated Allegra.

"I fell asleep before the storm came on."

"Fell asleep—out-of-doors—and at sunset! What dreadful imprudence."

"I went out too late, I'm afraid; but I was so tired of waiting for you. A kind of horror of the house and the silence came upon me—and I felt I must go out into the woods. I walked too far—and fell asleep from sheer fatigue; and when I woke I saw a yacht fighting with the wind. I'm afraid she'll go down."

"What, you noticed her too?" exclaimed Hulbert. "I didn't think you cared enough about yachts to take notice of her. I was watching her as we came down the hill; rather too much canvas; but she's right enough. She's past Arma di Taggia by this time, I dare say. I'll go and look for Disney, and tell him you're safe and sound. Perhaps I shall miss him in the wood. It's like a Midsummer Night's Dream, isn't it, Allegra?" he said, laughing, as he went out of the gate.

"If it were only midsummer, I shouldn't

care," answered his sweetheart, with her arm round Isola, who stood beside her, pale and shivering. "Come in, dear, and let me make you warm, if I can."

" If they should all go down in the darkness!" said Isola, in a low, dreamy voice. "The boat looked as if it might be wrecked at any moment."

Allegra employed all her arts as a sick-nurse in the endeavour to ward off any evil consequence from that imprudent slumber in the chill hour of sunset; but her cares were unavailing. Isola was restless and feverish all night, yet she insisted on getting up at her usual hour next morning, and declared herself quite capable of the journey to Genoa. Allegra and her brother, however, insisted on her resting for a day or two. So the departure was postponed, and the doctor sent for. He advised at least three days' rest, with careful nursing; and he reproved his patient severely for her imprudence in exposing herself to the evening air.

Captain Hulbert appeared at tea-time, just returned from a railway journey to Allassio.

" I've a surprise for you, Mrs. Disney," he said, seating himself by the sofa where Isola was lying, surrounded by invalid luxuries, books, lemonade, fan, and eau de Cologne flask, her feet covered with a silken rug.

"A surprise!" she echoed faintly, as if life held no surprises for her. "What can that be?"

"You remember the yacht you saw last night?"

"Yes," she cried, roused in an instant, and clasping her hands excitedly. "Did she go down?"

"Not the least little bit. She is safe and sound at Allassio. She is called the *Eurydice*, she hails last from Syracuse, and my brother is on board her. He wired to me this morning to go over and see him. I'm very glad I went, for he is off to Corfu to-morrow. The *Flying Dutchman* isn't in it with him."

There was a curious silence. Martin Disney was sitting on the other side of his wife's sofa, where he had been reading selected bits of the *Times*, such portions of the news of men and nations as he fancied might interest her. Allegra was busy with a piece of delicate needle-work, and did not immediately reply; but it was she who was first to speak.

"How frightened you would have been yester-day evening had you known who was on board the boat," she said.

"I don't know about being frightened, but he was certainly carrying too much canvas. I told him so this morning."

"What did he say?"

"Laughed at me. 'You sailors never believe that a landsman can sail a ship,' he said. I wanted to talk to his sailing-master, but he told me he was his own sailing-master. If his ship was doomed to go down, he meant to be at the helm himself."

"That sounds as if he were foolhardy," said Allegra.

"I told him I did not like the rig of his boat, nor the name of his boat, and I reminded him how I saw the *Eurydice* off Portland with all her canvas spread the day she went down. I was with the Governor of the Prison, a naval man, who had been commander on my first ship, and we stood side by side on the cliff, and watched her as she went by. 'If this wind gets much stronger, that ship will go down,' said my old captain, 'unless they take in some of their canvas.' And a few hours later these poor fellows had all gone to the bottom. I asked Lostwithiel why he called his boat the *Eurydice*. 'Fancy,' he said; he had a fancy for the name. 'I've never forgotten the old lines we used to hammer out when we were boys,' he said—' "Ah, miseram, Eurydicen, anima fugiente vocabat; Eurydicen toto referebant flumine ripæ." ' "

"I don't think the name matters, if she is a good boat," said Allegra, with her calm common-sense.

"Well, she is, and she isn't. She is a finer boat than the *Vendetta*; but I'd sooner handle the *Vendetta* in a storm. There are points about his new boat that I don't quite like. However, he had her built by one of the finest builders on the Clyde, and it will be hard if she goes wrong. He has given me the *Vendetta* as a wedding-present—in advance of the event—on condition that I sink her when I'm tired of her; and he said he hoped she'd be luckier to me than she has been to him."

Martin Disney sat silent by his wife's sofa. He could never hear Lord Lostwithiel's name without a touch of pain. His only objection to

Hulbert as a brother-in-law was the thought that
the two men were of the same race—that he
must needs hear the hated name from time to
time; and yet he believed his wife's avowal that
she was pure and true. His hatred of the name
came only from the recollection that she had
been slandered by a man whom he despised.
He looked at the wasted profile on the satin
pillow, so wan, so transparent in its waxen pallor,
the heavy eyelid drooping languidly, the faintly
coloured lips drawn as if with pain—a broken
lily. Was this the kind of woman to be suspected of evil—this fair and fragile creature, in
whom the spiritual so predominated over the
sensual? He hated himself for having been for
a moment influenced by that underbred scoundrel
at Glenaveril, for having been base enough to
doubt his wife's purity.

He had pained and humiliated her, and now
the stamp of death was on the face he adored,
and before him lay the prospect of a life's
remorse.

They left San Remo three days afterwards,
Isola being pronounced able to bear the journey,
though her cough had been considerably in-

creased by that imprudent slumber in the wood. She was anxious to go; and doctor and husband gave way to her eagerness for new scenes.

"I am so tired of this place," she said piteously. "It is lovely; but it is a loveliness that makes me melancholy. I want to be in a great city where there are lots of people moving about. I have never lived in a city, but always in quiet places—beautiful, very beautiful, but so still—so still—so full of one's self and one's own thoughts."

CHAPTER IX.

ECCO ROMA.

THE agent had proved himself worthy of trust, and had chosen the lodging for Colonel Disney's family with taste and discretion. It was a first floor over a jeweller's shop in a short street behind the Piazza di Spagna, and under the Pincian Gardens. There were not too many stairs for Isola to ascend when she came in from her drive or walk. The gardens were close at hand, and all around there were trees and flowers, and an atmosphere of verdure and retirement in the midst of the great cosmopolitan city.

It was dusk when the train came into the terminus; and Isola was weary and exhausted after the long hot journey from Pisa, the glare of the sun, and the suffocating clouds of dust, and the beautiful monotony of blue sea and

sandy plains, long level wastes, where nothing
grew but brushwood and osier, and stretches of
marshy ground, with water pools shining here
and there, like burnished steel, and distant islets
dimly seen athwart a cloud of heat. Then
evening closed in, and it was through a grey and
formless world that they approached the city
whose very name thrilled her.

The railway station was very much like all the
other great termini; like Milan, like Genoa.
There was the same close rank of omnibuses.
There were the same blue blouses and civil,
eager porters, piling up the innumerable pack-
ages of the Italian traveller, loading themselves
like so many human beasts of burden, and with
no apparent limit to their capacity for carrying
things. Two flys were loaded with the miscel-
laneous luggage, and then Isola was handed to
her place in another, with Allegra by her side,
and through the narrow streets of tall houses,
under the dim strip of soft April night, she
drove through the city of heroes and martyrs,
saints and apostles, wicked emperors and holy
women, the city of historical contrasts, of darkness and light, refinement and barbarism, of all

things most unlike each other, from Nero to Paul, from Domitian to Gregory the Great.

The glory and the beauty of Rome only began to dawn upon her next morning, in the vivid sunlight, when she climbed the steps of the Trinita de' Monte, and then with Allegra's arm to lean upon went slowly upward and again upward to the topmost terrace on the Pincian Hill, and stood leaning on the marble balustrade, and gazing across the city that lay steeped in sunshine at her feet—over palace and steeple, pinnacle and tower, to the rugged grandeur of Hadrian's Tomb, and to that great dome whose vastness makes all other things seem puny and insignificant. This was her first view of the world's greatest church.

The air was clear and cool upon this height, although the city below showed dimly through a hazy veil of almost tropical heat. Everywhere there was the odour of summer flowers, the overpowering sweetness of lilies of the valley, and great branches of lilac, white and purple, brimming over in the baskets of the flower-sellers.

On such a morning as this one could understand how the Romans came to call April the joyous month, and to dedicate this season of sunshine and flowers to the Goddess of Beauty and Love.

Isola's face lighted up with a new gladness, a look of perfect absorption and self-forgetfulness, as she leant upon the balustrade, and gazed across that vast panorama, gazed and wondered, with eyes that seemed to grow larger in their delight.

"And is this really Rome?" she murmured softly.

"Yes, this is Rome," cried Allegra. "Isn't it lovely? Isn't it all you ever dreamt of or hoped for? And yet people have so maligned it— called it feverish, stuffy, disappointing, dirty! Why, the air is ether—inspiring, health-giving! April in Rome is as fresh as April in an English forest; only it is April with the warmth and flowers of June. I feel sure you will grow ever so much stronger after one little week in Rome."

"Yes, I know I shall be better here. I feel better already," said Isola, with a kind of feverish hopefulness. "It was so good of Martin to bring me. San Remo is always lovely—and I shall love it to the end of my life, because it was my first home in Italy—but I was beginning to be a little tired—not of the olive woods and the sea, but of the people we met, and the sameness of life. One day was so like another."

"It was monotonous, of course," agreed Allegra; "and being a little out of health, you would be bored by monotony sooner than Martin or I. It was such a pity you did not like the yacht. That made such a change for us. The very olive woods and the mountain villages seem new when one sees them from the water. I was never tired of looking at the hills between San Remo and Bordighera, or the promontory of Monaco, with its cathedral towers. It was a pleasure lost to you, dear; but it could not be helped, I suppose. Yet once upon a time you used to be so fond of the sea, when you and I went in our row-boat, tempting danger round by Neptune Point."

"I may have been stronger then," Isola faltered.

"Oh, forgive me, darling! What an inconsiderate wretch I am ! But Rome will give you

back your lost strength; and we shall round
Neptune Point again, and feel the salt spray
dashing over our heads as we go out into the
great fierce Atlantic. I confess that sometimes,
when that divine Mediterranean which we are
never tired of worshipping has been lying in the
sunshine like one vast floor of *lapis lazuli*, I have
longed for something rougher and wilder—for
such a sea as you and I have watched from the
Rashleigh Mausoleum."

Colonel Disney and his wife and sister went
about in a very leisurely way in their explorations. In the first place, he was very anxious
to avoid anything approaching fatigue for his
wife; and in the second place it was only the
beginning of April, and they were to be in
Rome for at least a month; there was therefore
no need for rushing hither and thither at the
tourist pace, with guide-books in their hands,
and anxious, heated countenances, perspiring
through the streets, and suffering deadly chills
in the churches. Allegra's first desire was
naturally to see the picture-galleries, and to
these she went for the most part alone, leaving
Isola and her husband free to wander about

as they pleased, upon a friendly equality of ignorance, knowing very little more than Childe Harold and Murray could teach them. Isola's Rome was Byron's Rome.

There was one spot she loved better than any other in the city of mighty memories. It was not hallowed by the blood of saint or hero, sage or martyr. It had no classical associations. He whose heart lay buried there under the shadow of the tribune's mighty monument, perished in the pride of manhood, in the freshness and glory of life; and that heart—so warm and generous to his fellow-men — had hardened itself against the God of saint and martyr, the God of Peter and Paul, Lawrence and Gregory, Benedict and Augustine. Yet for Isola there was no grave in Rome so fraught with spiritual thoughts as Shelley's grave, no sweeter memory associated with the eternal city than the memory of his wanderings and meditations amidst the ruined walls of the Baths of Caracalla, where his young genius drank in the poetry of the long past, and fed upon the story of the antique dead.

She came to Shelley's grave as often as she

could steal away from the anxious companions of her drives and walks.

"I like to be alone now and then," she told her husband. "It rests me to sit by myself for an hour or two in this lovely place."

There was a coachman in the Piazza who was in the habit of driving Colonel Disney's family —an elderly man, sober, steady and attentive, with intelligence that made him almost as good as a guide. He was on the watch for his English clients every morning. They had but to appear on the Piazza, and he was in attendance, ready to take them to the utmost limit of a day's journey, if they liked. Were they in doubt where to go, he was always prompt with suggestions.

He would drive Isola to the door of the English cemetery, leave her there, and return at her bidding to drive her home again. Disney knew she was safe when this veteran had her in charge. The man was well known in the Piazza, and of established character for honesty. She took a book or two in her light basket, buying a handful of flowers here and there from the women and children as she went along, till

the books were hidden under roses and lilac.
The custodian of the cemetery knew her, and
admitted her without a word. He had watched
her furtively once or twice, to see that she
neither gathered the flowers nor tried to scratch
her name upon the tombs. He had seen her
sitting quietly by the slab which records Shelley's
death—and the death of that faithful friend
who was laid beside him, sixty years afterwards.
Sixty years of loving, regretful memory, and
then union in the dust. Shall there not be a
later and a better meeting, when those two
shall see each other's faces and hear each other's
voices again, in a world where old things shall
be made new, where youth and its wild freshness
shall come back again, and Trelawney shall
be as young in thought and feeling as Shelley?

The English burial-place was a garden of
fairest flowers at this season—a paradise of roses
and clematis, azaleas and camelias—and much
more beautiful for its wilder growth of trailing
foliage and untended shrubs, the pale cold blue
of the periwinkle that carpeted slope and bank,
and for the background of old grey wall, severe
in its antique magnificence, a cyclopean rampart,

relic of time immemorial, clothed and beautified with weed and floweret that grew in every cleft and cranny.

Here, in a sheltered angle to the left of the poet's grave, Isola could sit unobserved, even when the custodian brought a party of tourists to see the hallowed spot, which occurred now and then while she sat there. The tourists for the most part stared foolishly, made some sentimental remark if they were women, or if they were men, betrayed a hopeless ignorance of the poet's history, and not unfrequently confounded him with Keats. Isola sat half-hidden in her leafy corner, where the ivy and the acanthus hung from the great grey buttress against which she leant, languid, half-dreaming, with two books on her lap.

One was her Shelley—her much-read Shelley —a shabby, cloth-bound volume, bought in her girlhood at the bookseller's in the Place Duguesclin, where English books could be got by special order, and at special prices. The other was an Italian Testament, which her husband had bought her at San Remo, and in which she had read with extreme diligence and

with increasing fervour as her soul became more
deeply moved by Father Rodwell's sermons. It
was not that she had ever been one of those
advanced thinkers who will accept no creed
which does not square with their own little
theories and fit in to their own narrow circle
of possibilities. She had never doubted the
creed she had been taught in her childhood,
but she had thought very little about serious
things, since she was a young girl, preparing
for her confirmation, touched with girlish enthusiasm, and very much in earnest. In these
fair spring days, and in this city of many
memories, all young thoughts had re-awakened
in her mind. She pored over the familiar
Gospel-stories, and again, as in the first freshness of her girlhood, she saw the sacred figure
of the Redeemer and Teacher in all the vivid
light and colour of a reality, close at hand.
Faith stretched across the abyss of time, and
brought the old world of the Gospel-story close
to her; the closer, because she was in Rome,
not far from that church which enshrines the
print of the Divine footstep, when He who was
God and Man, appeared to His disciple, to

foreshadow approaching martyrdom, to inspire the fortitude of the martyr. Yes, although the Saviour's earthly feet never entered the city, every hill and every valley within and without those crumbling walls has interwoven itself so closely with the story of His life—through the work of His saints and martyrs—that it is nowise strange if the scenes and images of the sacred story seem nearer and more vivid in Rome than in any other place on earth, not excepting Jerusalem. It was from Rome, not from Jerusalem, that the Cross went out to the uttermost ends of the world. It is the earth of the Colosseum and the Borgo that is steeped in the blood of those who have died for Christ. It was Rome that ruled the world, through the long night of barbarism and feudal power, by the invincible force of that one holy name.

It might seem strange that Isola should turn from the story of the Evangelists to the works of a poet whose human sympathies were so wrung by the evil that has been wrought in the name of the Cross that he was blind to the infinitely greater good which Christianity has accomplished for mankind. Shelley saw the blood of the martyrs, not as a sublime testimony to the God-like power of faith, not as a sacrifice rich in after-fruits, sad seed of a joyous harvest—but as the brutal outcome of man's cruelty, using any name, Christ, or Buddha, Mahomet, or Brahma—as the badge of tyranny, the sanction to torture and to slay.

Shelley's melancholy fate seemed brought nearer to her now that she sat beside his grave, in the summer stillness, and in the shadow of the old Aurelian Wall. It was only his heart which was lying there, that imperishable heart which Trelawney's hand snatched from the flame of the Greek pyre, from the smoke of pine-logs and frankincense, wine and oil. Sixty years had passed before that hand lay cold in the grave beside the buried heart of the poet, sixty years of severance, and fond faithful memory, before death brought reunion.

What a beautiful spirit this, which was so early quenched by the cruellest stroke of Fate—a light such as seldom shone out of mortal clay, a s͵ ʼ ͙ of fire and brightness, intangible, untamable, not to be shut within common limits, nor judged by common laws!

CHAPTER X.

OF the people who came to look upon the grave, some to lay a tributary flower upon the stone, and some to pluck a leaf or two of acanthus or violet, all hitherto had been strangers to Isola, had gone away without seeing her, or had glanced indifferently, as at one more unfortunate with a sketching-block, spoiling paper in the pursuit of the unattainable. There were so many amateur artists sitting about in the outskirts of the city, that such a figure in a romantic spot challenged nobody's attention. So far people had come and gone, and had taken no notice; but one afternoon a figure in a long black cassock came suddenly between her and the golden light, and Isola looked up with a cry of surprise on recognizing Father Rodwell.

"You did not expect to see me here," he said, holding out his hand.

She had risen from her seat on the low grassy bank, and she gave him her hand, half in pleasure, half in a nervous apprehension which his keen eye was quick to perceive. His life had been spent in dealings with the souls of men and women, and he had learnt to read those living pages as easily as he read Plato or Spinosa.

"No," she said. "I had no idea you were in Rome. You told us you were going back to London."

"I meant to go back to London and hard work, but my doctor insisted upon my prolonging my holiday for a few weeks, so I came here instead. Rome always draws me, and is always new. Rome gives me fresh life and fresh power when my heart and brain have been feeling benumbed and dead. I am glad they brought you here, Mrs. Disney. You were looking languid and ill when you left San Remo. I hope Rome has revivified you."

He looked at her earnestly. Her face had been in shadow until now, but as she moved into the sunlight, he saw that the lines had sharpened in the pale, wan face, and that there was the stamp of wasting disease in the hollow cheeks, and about the sunken eyes, and in the almost bloodless lips. As he looked at her in friendliest commiseration those pathetic grey eyes—whose expression had baffled his power of interpretation hitherto—filled suddenly with tears, and in the next moment she clasped her hands before her face in an agony of grief.

The Italian Testament which she had been reading when he approached dropped at her feet, and stooping to pick it up Father Rodwell saw that it was open at the fourth chapter of St. John, the story of the woman of Samaria, she with whom Christ talked at the well. A leaf from Shelley's grave lay upon the book, as if to mark where she had been reading, and Father Rodwell's quick glance saw that the page was blotted with tears.

"My dear Mrs. Disney," he said gently, "is there anything wrong at home? Your husband, your boy are well, I hope?"

"Yes, thank God, they are both well. God has been very good to me. He might have taken those I love. He has been very merciful."

"He is merciful to all His creatures; though there are times when His dealings with us seem very hard. But we know that we look through a glass, darkly, and it needs the light of faith to pierce the shadows that close us round. Oh, Mrs. Disney, you can't think how difficult a priest's office is sometimes when he has to reconcile the afflicted with the Providence that has seen fit to lay some heavy burden on them. They cannot understand; they cannot say it is well. They cannot kiss the rod. But as you say, God has been very good to you. Your lines have been set in pleasant places. You are hedged round and sheltered by love. I never saw greater affection in husband for wife than I have seen in your husband. I never saw sister more devoted to sister than your sister-in-law is to you."

She had sunk again into a sitting position on the low bank at the foot of the wall. Her face was still hidden, and her sobs came faster as he spoke to her.

"Why should you grieve at the thought of their love? Is it because it may please God to take you from them in the morning of your life? If it is that dread which agitates you I entreat you to put it aside. There is nothing in your case that forbids hope, and hope will do much to help your recovery. You should tell yourself how valuable your life is to those who love you. The thought of their affection should give you courage to struggle against apathy and languor. Believe me, invalids have their condition a great deal more in their own power than they are inclined to believe. So much can be overcome where the spirit is strong and brave, where faith and hope fight against bodily weakness. You ought not to be sitting alone here in this saddening spot. It is lovely, but with the beauty of death. You ought to be driving out to Frascati or to Tivoli with your husband. You ought to be watching the carriages in the Pincian Gardens, or amusing yourself in one of the picture-galleries.

"I had rather be alone," she said, wiping away her tears, and in some degree recovering her self-possession.

"That is a morbid fancy, and one that hinders your recovery."

"I have no wish to recover. I only want to die."

"My dear Mrs. Disney, it is your duty to fight against these melancholy moods. Can you be indifferent to your husband's feelings? Have you not the mother's natural desire to watch over your child's early years, to see him reach manhood?"

"No, no, no!" she cried passionately. "I have had enough of life. They are dear to me, very dear. No wife ever loved and honoured her husband more than I love and honour mine—but it is all over, it is past, and ended. I am more than resigned to death—I am thankful that God has called me away."

He watched her closely as she spoke, watched her with his hand upon hers, which was cold as ice. He had heard such words before from the early doomed, but they had been accompanied by religious exaltation; they had been the outpouring of a faith that saw the gates of heaven opened and the Son of man sitting in glory—of a love that longed to be with God. Here there was no sign of hope or exaltation. There were only the tokens of despair.

He remembered how agitated he had seen her many times in the little church at San Remo, and how, although hanging eagerly upon his preaching, she had persistently avoided anything like serious conversation with him upon the few occasions when he had found himself alone with her.

He had her Testament still in his hand, and looking down at the tear-stained page it seemed to him that there lay the clue to her melancholy.

"You have been reading the story of the woman of Samaria," he said.

"Yes."

"And you have read that other story of her who knelt in the dust at her Saviour's feet, and to whom He said, 'Neither do I condemn thee.'"

"Yes."

"Is there anything in either of those stories to sadden you more than the thought of sin and sorrow saddens all of us?"

She looked at him shrinkingly, pale as death, as if he had a dagger, in his hand ready to strike her.

"No, I don't suppose there is anything that goes home to my heart any more than to other hearts," she said, after a pause, trying to speak carelessly. "We are all sinners. The Gospel teaches us that in every line! We are none of us altogether worthy—not even my husband, I suppose, although to me he seems a perfect Christian."

"I can believe that he is a Christian, Mrs. Disney, and a man of strong convictions. If he had wronged anybody, I do not think he would rest till he had atoned for that wrong."

"I am sure he would not. He would do his uttermost to atone. And so would I—although I do not pretend to be half so good a Christian as he is. I would do all in my power to atone for any wrong I had done to one I loved."

"As you love your husband, for instance."

"Yes, as I love him. He is first in the world for me. Dear as my child is, Martin must always be first."

"And you would not for the world do him any wrong?" pursued the priest, more and more earnest as he went on, pale with emotion, his whole power of observation concentrated upon the whitening face and lowered eyelids of the woman sitting at his feet.

"Not for the world, not for my life," she said,

with her hands tightly clasped, her eyes still hidden under the heavy lids, tearless now—and with dry and quivering lips, from which the words came with a dull and soulless sound. "I would die to save him an hour's pain. I would fling away this wretched life rather than grieve him for a moment."

"Poor soul!" murmured the priest, pitying that debt of self-abasement which he understood so well, under whatsoever guise she might hide her contrition. "Poor soul, you talk too lightly of that great mystery which we should all face in a spirit of deep humility. Do you feel that you can contemplate that passage through death to a new life without fear of the issue? Have you no reckoning to make with the God who pardons repentant sinners? Do you stand before Him with a clear conscience—having kept nothing back—cherished no hidden sin?"

"No one can be without sin in His sight. Do you suppose that I am sinless, or that I have ever believed myself sinless? I know how weak and poor a thing I am—a worm in the sight of Him who rules the universe. But if—if He cares for such as I, He knows that I am sorry for every sinful thought and every sinful act of my life."

She spoke in short sentences, each phrase broken by a stifled sob. She felt as if he were tearing out her heart, this man who had been heretofore so kindly and indulgent in his speech and manner that he seemed to make religion an easy thing, a garment as loose and expansive as philosophy itself. And, now, all at once he appeared before her as a judge, searching out her heart, cruel, inflexible, weighing her in the balance, and finding her wanting.

"If I am sorry," she murmured, between her sobs, "what more can God or man require of me?"

"Nothing, if your sorrow is that true sorrow which means repentance, and goes hand-in-hand with atonement. Forgive me, my dear friend, for presuming to speak unreservedly to you. If I try to find out the nature of your wound it is only that I may help you to heal it. Ever since I have known you I have seen the tokens of a wounded heart, a bruised and broken spirit. I saw you surrounded with all the blessings that make woman's lot happy. It was hardly possible to conceive fairer surroundings and truer friends. Can you wonder, then, if my compassionate interest was awakened by the indications of a deep-rooted sorrow for which there was no apparent cause? I saw your emotion in church, saw how quickly your heart and mind responded to the appeal of religion—saw in you a soul attuned to heavenly things, and day by day my interest in you and yours grew stronger. The hope of seeing you again, of helping you to bear your secret burden, of ultimately lightening it, was one of my reasons for coming to Rome. I felt somehow that you and I had not met in vain—that my power to move you was not without a meaning in both our lives; that if, as I thought, you needed spiritual help and comfort, it was my vocation to help and comfort you. And so I came to Rome, and so I found out where you spent your quiet hours, and so I have followed you here this afternoon. Tell me, Mrs. Disney, did I presume too much? Was it the preacher's vanity or the priest's intuition that spoke?"

"It was intuition," she said. "You saw that I had sinned. None but a sinner could shed such tears—could so feel the terror of God's wrath."

"It is of His love I want you to think. Of His immeasurable love and pity. Of His Son's Divine compassion. If you have any special need of His pardon; if there is any sinful secret locked in your heart; do not let the golden hours go by—the time meet for repentance."

"I have repented," she cried piteously. "My life has been one long repentance ever since my sin."

"And your husband—he who so fondly loves you—he knows all, and has forgiven all?"

"Knows!" The word broke from her lips almost in a shriek of horror. "He knows nothing —he must never know. He would despise me, leave me to die alone, while he went far away from me, to the very end of the world. He would take his son with him. I should be left alone— alone to face death—the most desolate creature God ever looked upon. Oh, Father Rodwell, why have you wrung my secret from me?" she cried, grovelling on her knees in the long grass beside him, clinging to his hand as he bent over her, gravely compassionate, deeply moved by her distress. "How cruel to question—to torture me—how cruel to use your power of reading guilty hearts.   You will tell my husband, who so loves and trusts me.   You will tell him what a guilty wretch I am."

"Tell him, Mrs. Disney!   Can you forget that I am a priest—in whose heart the sinner's secret is buried as in a grave?   Do you think I have never talked with the tempted and the sorrowing before to-day?   Do you think that grief such as yours can be an unknown experience to a man who has worked in a crowded London parish for nearly twenty years?   I wanted to know the worst, so that I might be able to advise and to console you.   If I have questioned you to-day, it has been as a priest has the right to question ; and this place where you and I have met to-day is in my sight as sacred as the confessional.   You need have no fear that I shall tell your husband the secret of your sorrow.   All I will do is to help you to find strength to tell him yourself."

"Oh no, no, no !" she cried piteously.   "Never ! never !   I can die, I am prepared to die ; but I can never tell him—I cannot, I dare not."

"Yet you could dare to die with a lie upon your lips—you who are ready to meet your Judge —you whose whole life is a lie—you who have cheated and betrayed the best of men. Oh, Mrs. Disney, reflect what this thing is which you are doing; reflect what kind of sin it is you are committing. If, as your own sorrowing words acknowledge, you have been a false wife—a false wife to the best and truest of husbands, can you dare to act out that falsehood to the last, to die with that guilty secret locked in your heart, from him who has a right to know,—and who alone upon earth has a right to pardon."

"Oh, how cruel you are!" she said, lifting up her streaming eyes to his earnest, inflexible face. "Is it a Christian's part to be so cruel, to break the bruised reed, to crush anything so weak and wretched as I am? Is not repentance enough? I have spent long nights in penitence and tears, long days in dull aching remorse. I would have given all my future life to atone for one dreadful hour—one unpremeditated yielding to temptation. I *have* given my life—for my secret has killed me. What more can man or God demand of me? What more can I do to win forgiveness?"

"Only this—tell your husband the truth—however painful, however humiliating the confession. That will be your best atonement. That is the sacrifice which will help to reconcile you with your God. You cannot hope for God's love and pardon hereafter, if you live and die as a hypocrite here. God's saints were some of them steeped in the darkness of guilt before they became the children of light—but there was not one of them who shrank from the confession of his sins."

"You are a man," sobbed Isola. "You do not know what it is for a woman to confess that she is unworthy of her husband's love. You do not know. It is not possible for a man to know the meaning of shame."

"You are wrong there," he said, gently lifting her from the ground, and placing her beside him on the bank. "What chastity is to a woman, honour is to a man. Men have had to stand up before their fellow-men and acknowledge their violation of man's code of honour; knowing that such acknowledgment made them dirt, and very dirt, in the sight of honourable men. You, as a woman, know not how deep men's scorn cuts a man who has sinned against the law which governs gentlemen. A woman thinks there is no such sting as the sting of her shame. Men know better. Yes, I know that it will be most bitter, more bitter than death—for you to tell Colonel Disney that you are not what you have seemed to him; but apart from all considerations of duty, do not his love and devotion deserve the sacrifice of self-love on your part? Can you bear yourself to the last, as a virtuous wife—enjoying his respect—knowing that it is undeserved—— "

"I will tell him—at the last," she faltered. "In that parting hour I shall not shrink from telling him all—how I sinned against him—almost unawares—drifting half unconsciously into a fatal entanglement—and then—and then—against my will—in my weakness and helplessness—alone in the power of the man I loved—betrayed into sin. Oh God! why do you make me remember?" she cried wildly, turning upon the priest in passionate reproachfulness. "For years I have been trying to forget—trying to blank out the past—praying, praying, praying that my humble, tearful love for my husband and my child might cancel those hours of sin. And you come to me, and question me, and on pretence of saving my soul, you force me to look back upon that bygone horror—to live again through that time of madness—the destruction of my life.   Cruel, cruel, cruel!"

"Forgive me!" said Father Rodwell, very gently, seeing that she was struggling with hysteria. "I have been too hard, perhaps, too eager to convince you of the right! There are some men, even of my sacred calling, who would judge your case otherwise—who would say the husband is happy in his ignorance; the wife has repented of her sin. *Non quieta movere.* But it is not in my nature to choose the easy pathways; and it may be that I am too severe a teacher. We will not talk any more about serious things to-day. Only believe that I am your friend—your sincere and devoted friend. If I have spoken hard things, be assured I would have spoken in the same spirit had you been my own sister. Let us say no more yet awhile—and perhaps when you have thought over our interview to-day you will come to see things almost as I see them, and of your own accord you will do that which I, as the minister of Christ's Gospel, would urge you to do. I won't press

the matter. I will leave your own heart and
conscience to plead with you. And now may I
walk home with you, before the beauty of the
afternoon begins to fade?"

"The vetturino will be waiting for me at the
gate," Isola answered, with a dull, dead voice,
rising languidly, and adjusting the loosened hair
about her forehead with tremulous fingers.

She had thrown off her hat a little while
before, and now she took it up, and straightened
the loops of ribbon with a nervous touch here
and there, and then put the hat on again, and
arranged the gossamer veil, which she hoped
might hide her swollen eyelids and tear-stained
cheeks.

"If Martin should come to meet me, what will
he think?" she said piteously.

"Let me go with you, and I may be able to
distract his attention—if you don't want him to
see that you have been crying."

"No, no. He must not see. He would wonder,
and question me—and guess, perhaps—as you
did just now. How was it you knew—what
made you guess?" she asked, with a sense of
rebellion against this man who had pierced the

veil behind which she had been hiding herself so long.

"I saw your sorrow; and I knew that there could scarcely be so deep a sorrow if there were no memory of sin. Will you take my arm down this steep path?"

"No, thank you. I know every step. I could walk about this place in my sleep. You have been cruel to me, Father Rodwell, very cruel. Promise me one thing by way of atonement for your cruelty. Promise me that if I die in Rome I shall be buried in this place, and as near Shelley's grave as they can find room to lay me."

"I promise. Yes, it is a sweet spot, is it not? It was down yonder in the old burial-ground that Shelley looked upon the grave of Keats, and said it was a spot to make one in love with death. But I would not have you think yourself doomed to an early death, Mrs. Disney. Have you never read in the 'Lives of the Saints' how some who were on the point of death have revived at the touch of the holy oil, and have lived and have renewed their strength, and re-entered the world to lead a holier and nobler life than they had led before? Who knows if you were to confess your sin, and patiently suffer whatever penance you were called upon to bear, new vistas might not open for you? There is more than one way of being happy in this world. If you could never again know the sweetness of a domestic life—as trusted wife and happy mother—there are other and wider lives in which you would count your children and your sisters by hundreds. There are sisterhoods in which your future might be full of usefulness and full of peace. Or if you had no vocation for that wider life, it might be that touched by your helplessness in the past, and your remorse in the present, your husband might find it in his heart to forgive that bygone sin, and still to cherish, and still to hold you dear."

"No, no," she cried impatiently. "I would not live for an hour after he knew. I know what he would do. He has told me. He would leave me—at once, and for ever. I should never see his face again. I should be dead to him, by a worse death than the grave; for he would only think of me to shudder at my name. Oh, Father Rodwell, Christianity must be a cruel creed if it can demand such a sacrifice from me.

What good can come of his knowing the truth? Only agony to him and shame and despair to me. Can that be good?"

"Truth is life, and falsehood is death," answered the priest, firmly. "You must choose your own course, Mrs. Disney; but there is one argument I may urge as a man of the world rather than as a priest. Nothing is ever hidden for very long in this life. There is no secret so closely kept that some one has not an inkling of it. Better your husband should hear the truth from you, in humble self-accusation, than that he should learn it later—perhaps after he has mourned you for years—from a stranger's lips."

"Oh, that would be horrible—too horrible. But I will confess to him; I will tell him everything—on my death-bed. Yes, when life is ebbing, when the end is close, I will tell him. He shall know what a false and perjured creature I am. I swore to him—swore before God that I was true and faithful—that I loved him and no other. And it was true, absolute truth, when I took that oath. My sin was a thing of the past. I had loved another, and I had let my love lead me into sin. And then my husband asked me if I had been true and pure always; always. 'Is that true, Isola? I call upon God to hear your answer,' he said. And I answered yes, it was true. I lied before God rather than lose my husband's love; and God heard me, and the blight of His anger has been upon me ever since, withering and consuming me."

They went down the steep pathway, Father Rodwell first, Isola following, between the crowded graves, the azaleas and camelias, purple veronica, and cream-white guelder rose, lilac and magnolia, and on either hand a wilderness of roses, red and white.

The shadows of the cypresses closed over them in that deep alley, and the twilight gloom might seem symbolic of the passage through death to life; for beyond the gates, and through a gap in the cypress screen, the level landscape and the city domes and bell-towers were shining in the yellow light of afternoon.

CHAPTER XI.

"OH, OLD THOUGHTS THEY CLING, THEY CLING!"

Colonel Disney and Allegra were both pleased to welcome Father Rodwell to their home in the great city ; pleased to find that his own rooms were close by in the Via Babuino, and that he was likely to be their neighbour for some weeks. His familiarity with all that was worth seeing in the city and its surroundings made him a valuable companion for people whose only knowledge had been gathered laboriously from books. Father Rodwell knew every picture and every statue in the churches and galleries. There was not a building in Christian or Pagan Rome which had not its history and its associations for the man who had chosen the city as the holiday ground of his busy life long before he left the university, and who had returned again and

again, year after year, to tread the familiar paths
and ponder over the old records. He had seen
many of those monuments of Republic and Empire
emerge from the heaped-up earth of ages; had
seen hills cut down, and valleys laid bare; some
picturesque spots made less picturesque; other
places redeemed from ruin. He had seen the
squalor and the romance of Mediæval Rome
vanish before the march of improvement; and
he had seen the triumph of the commonplace
and the utilitarian in many a scene where the
melancholy beauty of neglect and decay had once
been dear to him.

With such a guide it was delightful to loiter
amidst the Palace of the Cæsars, or tread the
quiet lanes and by-paths of the Aventine, that
historic hill from whose venerable church the
bearers of Christ's message of peace and love set
out for savage Britain. Allegra was delighted
to wander about the city with such a companion,
lingering long before every famous picture, finding out altar-pieces and frescoes which no guide-
book would have helped her to discover; sometimes disputing Father Rodwell's judgment upon
the artistic value of a picture; sometimes agree-

ing with him—always bright, animated, and intelligent.

Isola joined in these explorations as far as her strength would allow. She was deeply interested in the churches, and in the stories of priest and pope, saint and martyr, which Father Rodwell had to tell of every shrine and tomb, whose splendour might otherwise have seemed colourless and cold. There was a growing enthusiasm in the attention with which she listened to every record of that wonder-working Church which created Christian Rome in all its pomp and dignity of architecture, and all its glory of art. The splendour of those mighty basilicas filled her with an awful sense of the majesty of that religion which had been founded yonder in darkness and in chains, in Paul's subterranean prison—yonder in tears where Paul and Peter spoke the solemn words of parting—yonder in blood on the dreary road to Ostia, where the headsman's axe quenched the greatest light that had shone upon earth since the sacrifice of Calvary.

Isola went about looking at these things like a creature in a dream. These stupendous tabernacles impressed her with an almost insupportable sense of their magnitude. And with that awestricken sense of power in the Christian Church there was interwoven the humiliating consciousness of her own unworthiness; a consciousness sharpened and intensified by every word that Father Rodwell had spoken in that agonizing hour of her involuntary confession.

He was so kind to her, so gentle, so courteous in every word and act, that she wondered sometimes whether he had forgotten that miserable revelation; whether he had forgotten that she was one of the lost ones of this earth, a woman who had forfeited woman's first claim to man's esteem. Sometimes she found herself lifting her eyes to his face in an unpremeditated prayer for pity, as they stood before some exquisite shrine of the Madonna, and the ineffable purity in the sculptured face looking down at her struck like a sharp sword into her heart. That mute appeal of Isola's seemed to ask, " Has the Mother of Christ any pity for such a sinner as I ? "

Colonel Disney was full of thoughtfulness for his wife in all their going to and fro; and before their day's rambles were half done he would drive her to any quiet spot where she might choose to spend a restful hour in the afternoon sunshine—in this or that convent garden, in some shaded corner on the Aventine, or among the wild flowers that grow in such luxuriance amidst the colossal ruins on the Palatine. Her favourite resort was still the English cemetery, and she always begged to be set down within reach of that familiar gate, where the custodian knew her as well as if she had been some restless spirit whose body lay under one of those marble urns, and whose ghost passed in and out of the gate every day.

It was in vain that her husband or her sister offered to be her companion in these restful hours. She always made the same reply.

"I am better alone," she would say. "It does me good to be alone. I don't like being alone indoors—I get low-spirited and nervous—but I like to sit among the flowers, and to watch the lizards darting in and out among the graves. I am never dull there. I take a book with me; but I don't read much. I could sit there for hours in a summer dream."

Martin Disney made a point of giving way to her will in all small things. She might be capricious, she might have morbid fancies. That was no business of his. It was his part to indulge her every whim, and to make her in love with life. All that he asked of Heaven was to spin out that attenuated thread. All that he desired was to hold her and keep her for his own against Death himself.

The *Vendetta* was at Civita Vecchia, from which port her skipper frequently bore down upon Rome, distracting Allegra from her critical studies in the picture-galleries, and from her work in her own little studio, a light, airy room on the fourth floor, with a window looking over the Pincian Gardens. Captain Hulbert was a little inclined to resent Father Rodwell's frequent presence in the family circle, and his too accomplished guidance in the galleries. It was provoking to hear a man talk, with an almost Ruskinesque enthusiasm and critical appreciation, of pictures which made so faint an appeal to the seaman. Here and there John Hulbert could see the beauty and merit of a painting, and was really touched by the influence of supreme art; but of technical qualities he knew nothing, and could hardly distinguish one master from another, was as likely as not to take Titian for Veronese, or Veronese for Titian.

He looked with a sceptical eye at the Anglican priest's cassock and girdle. If Father Rodwell had been a Papist it would have been altogether a more satisfactory state of things; but an Anglican—a man who might preach the beauty of holy poverty and a celibate life one year and marry a rich widow the year after—a man bound only by his own wishes.

Had Allegra been a thought less frank—had she been a woman whom it was possible to doubt —the sailor would have given himself over to the demon of jealousy; but there are happily some women in whom truth and purity are so transparently obvious that even an anxious lover cannot doubt them. Allegra was such an one. No suspicion of coquetry ever lessened her simple womanliness. She was a woman of whom a man might make a friend; a woman whose feelings and meanings he could by no possibility mistake.

He had pleaded his hardest and pleaded in vain for a June wedding. Isola's state of health was too critical for the contemplation of any change in the family circle.

"She could not do without me, nor could Martin either," Allegra told her lover. "It is I who keep house and manage their money, and see to everything for them. Martin has been utterly helpless since this saddening anxiety began. He thinks of nothing but Isola, and her chances of recovery. I cannot leave him while she is so ill."

"Have you any hope of her ever being better, my dear girl?"

"I don't know. It has been a long and wearing illness."

"It is not illness, Allegra. It is a gradual decay. My fear is that she will never revive. There is no marked disease—nothing for medicine to fight against. Such cases as hers are the despair of doctors. A spring has been broken somehow in the human machine. Science cannot mend it."

Allegra was very much of her sweetheart's opinion.

The English doctor in Rome was as kind and attentive as the doctor at San Remo; but although he had not yet pronounced the case hopeless, he took a by no means cheerful view of his patient's condition. He recommended Colonel Disney to leave the city before the third week in May, and to take his wife to Switzerland, travelling by easy stages, and doing all he could to amuse and interest her. If on the other hand it were important for Colonel Disney to be in England, he might take his wife back to Cornwall in June. But in this case she must return to the south in October. Lungs and heart were both too weak for the risks of an English winter.

"We will not go back to England," decided Disney. "My wife is not fond of Cornwall. Italy has been a delight to her; and Switzerland will be new ground. God grant the summer may bring about an improvement!"

The doctor said very little, and promised nothing.

Closely as they watched her, with anxious loving looks, it may be that seeing her every day even their eyes did not mark the gradual decline of vitality—the inevitable advance of decay. She never complained; the cough that marked the disease which had fastened on her lungs since February was not a loud or seemingly distressing cough. It was only now and then, when she tried to walk uphill, or over-exerted herself in any way, that her malady became painfully obvious in the labouring chest, flushed cheek, and panting breath; but she made light even of these symptoms, and assured her husband that Rome was curing her.

Her spirits had been less equable since Father Rodwell's appearance. She had alternated between a feverish intensity and a profound dejection. Her changes of mood had been sudden and apparently causeless; and those who watched and cherished her could do nothing to dispel the gloom that often clouded over her. If she were questioned she could only say that she was tired. She would never admit any reason for her melancholy.

CHAPTER XII.

"WE'LL BIND YOU FAST IN SILKEN CORDS."

CAPTAIN HULBERT was not selfish enough to
plead for his personal happiness in the midst
of a household shadowed by the foreboding of
a great sorrow. Martin Disney's face as he
looked at his wife in those moments which too
plainly marked the rapid progress of decay, was
in itself enough to put a check upon a lover's
impatience. How could any man plead for his
own pleasure—for the roses and sunshine of life
—in the presence of that deep despair?

"He knows that he is doomed to lose her,"
thought Hulbert; "knows it, and yet tries to
hope. I never saw such intense, unquestioning
love. One asks one's self involuntarily about
any woman—Is she worth it?"

And then he thought of Allegra, truthful and

impulsive, strong as steel, transparent as crystal. Yes, such a woman as that was worth the whole of a man's heart—worthy that a man should live or die for her. But it seemed to him that to compare Isola with Allegra was to liken an ash sapling to an oak.

He resigned himself to his disappointment, talked no more of Venice and the starlit lagunes, the summer nights on the Lido, and quoted no more of Ruskin's rhapsodies; but he came meekly day after day to join in the family excursion, whatever it might be. He had enough and to spare of ecclesiastical architecture and of the old masters during those summer-like mornings and afternoons. He heard more than enough of the mad Cæsars and the bad Cæsars, of wicked Empresses and of low-born favourites, of despotism throned in the palace and murder waiting at the gate, of tyranny drunken with power long abused, and treason on the watch for the golden opportunity to change one profligate master for another, ready to toss up for the new Cæsar, and to accept the basest slave for master, would he but open the Imperial treasury wide enough to the Prætorian's rapacious hands.

"People gloat over these hoary old walls as if they would like to have lived under Caligula," said the sailor, with a touch of impatience, when Father Rodwell had been expatiating upon a little bit of moulding which decorated a fragment of staircase.

"It would have been at least a picturesque time to have lived in," said Allegra. "Existence must have been a series of pictures by Alma Tadema."

Captain Hulbert was startled out of his state of placid submission by the intervention of a most unexpected ally.

It was one of the hottest days there had been since they came to Rome—a day on which to cross the Piazza in front of St. Peter's was like plunging into a bath of molten gold; in which to enter the great Basilica itself was like going into an ice-house. Father Rodwell was not with them upon this particular morning. They were a party of four, and a roomy landau had been engaged to drive them to the Church of St. Paul beyond the walls, and thence to the tomb of Cecilia Metella. Isola and Allegra had made pilgrimages to the spot before to-day. It was a drive they both loved, a glimpse of the pastoral life outside the gates of the city, and a place for ever associated with the poet whose verse was written in their hearts.

They dawdled over a light luncheon of macaroni and Roman wine at a *café* near the great cold white church, and then they drove through the sandy lanes in the heat of the afternoon, languid all of them, and Isola paler and more weary-looking than she had been for some time. Her husband watched her anxiously, and wanted to go back to Rome, lest the drive should be too exhausting for her.

"No, no, I am not tired," she answered impatiently. "I would much rather go on. I want to see that grim old tower again," and then she quoted the familiar lines, dreamily, with a faint pleasure in their music—

> "Perchance she died in youth : it may be bowed
> With woes far heavier than the ponderous tomb
> That weighed upon her gentle dust."

"Besides," she added confusedly, "I want to have a little private talk with Captain Hulbert, while Allegra is busy with her everlasting memoranda in that dirty little sketch-book which is stuffed with the pictures of the future. May I ? "

She looked from her husband to Captain Hulbert pleadingly. The latter was first to answer.

" I am at your service, Mrs. Disney; ready to be interrogated, or lectured, or advised, whichever you like."

" I am not going to do either of the three. I am going to ask you a favour."

" Consider that to ask is to be obeyed."

They alighted in the road by the tomb a few minutes afterwards. Allegra's note-book was out immediately, a true artist's book, crammed with every conceivable form of artistic reminiscence.

" Go and talk," she said, waving her hand to Isola and Hulbert; and then she clambered up a bank opposite that tower of other days to get a vantage ground for her sketch.

She had made a score of sketches on the same spot, but there were always new details to jot down, new effects and ideas, on that vast level which frames the grandeur of Rome. Yonder the long slanting line of the aqueduct; here the living beauty of calm-fronted Roman oxen moving with stately paces along the dusty way, the incarnation of strength and majesty, patience and labour.

"Stay here and smoke your cigar, Martin," said Isola, "while Captain Hulbert and I go for a little stroll."

Her husband smiled at her tenderly, cheered by her unwonted cheerfulness. His days and hours alternated between hope and despair. This moment was a moment of hope.

"My dearest, you are full of mystery to-day," he said, "and I am as full of curiosity. But I can wait. Consider me a statue of patience, and take your time."

She put her hand through Hulbert's arm, and led him away from the other two, sauntering slowly along beside the grassy bank.

"I want to talk about your wedding," she said, as soon as they were out of hearing. "When are you and Allegra going to be married?"

"My dear Mrs. Disney, you know that I pledged myself to wait a year from the time of our engagement—a year from last Christmas— you must remember. That was to be my probation."

"Yes, I remember; but that is all foolishness—idle romance. Allegra knows that you love her. I don't think she could know it any better after another half-year's devotion on your part."

"I don't think she could know it better after another half century. I know I could never love her more than I do now. I know I shall never love her less."

"I believe that you are good and true," said Isola. "As true and—almost—as good as he is"—with a backward glance at her husband. "If I did not believe that I should not have thought of saying what I am going to say."

"I am honoured by your confidence in me."

"I love Allegra too well to hazard her happiness. I know she loves you—has never cared for any one else. She was heart-whole till she saw you. She had no more thought of love, or lovers, than a child. I want you to marry her soon, Captain Hulbert—very soon, before we leave Rome. Would you not like to be married in Rome?"

"I would like to be married in Kamtchatka, or Nova Zembla—or the worst of those places whose very names suggest all kinds of uncomfortableness. There is no dismallest corner of the earth which Allegra could not glorify and make dear. But, as you suggest, Rome is classic—Rome is mediæval—Rome is Roman Catholic. It would be a new sensation for a plain man like me to be married in Rome. I suppose it could not be managed in St. Peter's?"

"Oh, Captain Hulbert, I want you to be serious."

"I am serious. Why, this is a matter of life or death to me. But I pleaded so hard for a June wedding—and to no purpose. I talked with the artfulness of the first Tempter—I tried to play upon her vanities as an artist. All in vain!"

"Tell her that I have set my heart upon seeing her married," said Isola, in a low voice.

"Why, of course, you will see her married, whether she be married in Rome or at Trelasco. That is no argument."

"But it is; indeed it is. Tell her that, if I am to be at her wedding, it must be soon, very soon. Life is so uncertain at best—and, although

I feel well and strong, sometimes—to-day, for instance—there are other times when I think the end is nearer than even my doctor suspects. And I know by his face that he does not give me a long lease of life."

"My dear Mrs. Disney, this is morbid. I am grieved to hear you talk in such a strain."

"Don't notice that. Don't say anything depressing to Allegra. I want her to go off to her Venetian honeymoon very happily—with not one cloud in her sky. She has been so good and dear to me. It would be hard if I could not rejoice in her happiness. I have rejoiced in it always; I shall take pleasure in it to the end of my life. It is the one unclouded spot——" She stopped with a troubled air. "Yes, it is a happy fate—to have cared for one, and one only, and to be loved again. Will you do what I ask you, Captain Hulbert? will you hurry on the wedding—for my sake?"

"I would do anything difficult and unwelcome for your sake—how much more will I hasten my own happiness—if I can. But Allegra is a difficult personage—as firm as rock when she has once made up her mind. And she has made up her mind to stay with you till you are quite well and strong again."

"She need not leave me for ever, because she marries. She can come back to me after a long honeymoon. We can all meet in Switzerland in August—if—if I go there with Martin, as he proposes."

"Well, I will try to bend that stubborn will."

"And you don't mind having a quiet wedding, if she consents to a much earlier date?"

"Mind? The quieter the better for me! I think a smart wedding is a preventive of matrimony. That sounds like a bull. I will say I think there are many wretched bachelors walking about who might have been happily married if it had not been for the fear of a smart wedding. We will have as quiet a wedding as you and Disney can desire; but I should like Lostwithiel to be present. He is my only near relation, and I don't want to cut him on the happiest day of my life. Why, Mrs. Disney, you are trembling! You have agitated yourself about this business; you have talked too much for your strength. Let me take you back to the carriage."

"Presently—yes, yes. The heat overcame me

for a moment, that's all. Would you mind not waiting for Lord Lostwithiel? I want the marriage to be at once—directly—as soon as Father Rodwell can get it arranged. And you don't know where a telegram would reach your brother?"

"Indeed, I do not; but by speculating a few messages of inquiry I could soon find out the whereabouts of the *Eurydice*."

"Don't wait for that. There would be delay. There must be delay if you have to consult any distant person's convenience. We are all here —you and Allegra, and Martin and I—and Father Rodwell would like to marry you. What do you want with anybody else?"

"Upon my word, I think you are right! Allegra is a creature of impulse—where principle is not at stake. If I asked her to marry me six weeks hence she would parley and make terms. If I ask her to marry me in a few days—before we leave Rome—she may consent. Have you talked to your husband? Is he of your opinion?"

"I have said nothing to him; but I know he would be pleased to see you and Allegra bound together for life."

"I will talk to him this afternoon. One can get everything one wants in Rome, I believe, from a papal dispensation down to an English solicitor. If we can but rattle through some kind of marriage settlement to your husband's satisfaction we can be married on the earliest day to which my darling will consent. God bless you, Mrs. Disney, for your unselfish thought of other people's happiness! You are not like most invalids, who would let a sister languish in lifelong spinsterhood rather than lose her as a nurse. God grant that your unselfishness may be recompensed by speedy recovery!"

"There will be a weight off my mind when you and Allegra are married," said Isola, gravely.

They walked slowly back to the spot where they had left their companions. A pair of oxen, with an empty cart, were standing in the road below the tomb, their driver lounging across the rough vehicle—man and beasts motionless as marble. Allegra sat on a hillock opposite, sketching the group. She had bribed the man to draw up for a brief halt while she made her rough sketch. The massive heads were drooping under the afternoon sun ; the tawny and cream-hued coats were stained with dust and purpled with the sweat of patient labour. The creatures looked as gracious and as wise as if they had been gods in disguise.

"Now, Allegra," said her brother, emptying the ashes out of his pipe, "are you ready to go home?"

"Yes, I have just jotted down what will serve to remind me of those splendid beasts; but I should like to have them standing there all day, so that I could paint them seriously. They are the finest models I have seen in Rome. Have you two quite finished your secrets and mysteries?" she asked, smiling at Isola, who was looking brighter than usual.

"Yes; I have said all I had to say, and have been answered as I wished to be answered. I shall go home very happy."

"That's a good hearing," said Disney, as he helped her into the landau.

Allegra had talked of wanting to revisit Caracalla's Baths, a wish of which Isola reminded her as they drove back to the city, along the

Appian Way: whereupon Captain Hulbert suggested that he and his sweetheart should stop to explore the ruins, while Disney and Isola went home.

Allegra blushed and consented, always a little shy at being alone with her lover, especially since he had pleaded so earnestly for a summer honeymoon.

"Mrs. Disney, your right place in Rome would be the Embassy," murmured Hulbert as he shut the carriage door; "you are a born diplomatist."

"What makes my dearest look so pleased and happy this afternoon?" asked Disney, as he changed to the seat beside his wife.

"I am glad because I think Captain Hulbert will persuade Allegra to marry him before we leave Rome. I begged him to hasten their marriage. That was my mystery, Martin. That was what he and I were talking about."

"But why wish to hasten matters, dear? They are very happy as it is—and a year is not a long engagement."

"Too long for me, Martin. I want to see her happy—I want to see them married before——"

" Before what, dear love ? " he asked tenderly.

" Before we leave Rome."

" That would be very short work. We leave in a fortnight. The weather will be growing too hot for you if we linger later."

" Yes, but everything can be settled in less time than that. Ask Father Rodwell. He knows Rome so well that he can help you to arrange all details."

" I thought that every young woman required at least six months for the preparation of her trousseau ? "

" Not such a girl as Allegra. She is always well dressed, and her wardrobe is the perfection of neatness—but she is not the kind of girl with whom new clothes are the distinctive feature of marriage. I don't think the trousseau will create any difficulty."

" And when she is gone, what will you do without your devoted companion ? Who will nurse you and take care of you ? "

" Löttchen or any other servant," she answered, with a kind of weary indifference. " It would be very hard if my bad health should stand in the way of Allegra's happiness. So long as you will stay with me and be kind to me, Martin, I need no one else."

Tears were streaming down her cheeks as she turned from him, pretending to be interested in the convent walls on the edge of the hill below which they were driving.

"So long as I stay with you! My darling, do you think business or pleasure, or any claim in this world, will ever take me away from you any more? All your hours are precious to me, Isola. I hardly live when I am away from you. Where-ever your doctor may send you, or your own fancy may lead you, I shall go with you, un-hesitatingly—without one regret for anything I leave behind."

"Don't say these things," she cried suddenly, with a choking sob; "you are too good to me. There are times when I can't bear it."

CHAPTER XIII.

"SO, FULL CONTENT SHALL HENCEFORTH BE MY LOT."

ALLEGRA was not inexorable. There, in the ruins of the Imperial baths, where Shelley dreamed the wonder-dream of his Prometheus, Captain Hulbert pleaded his cause. Could love resist the pleading of so fond a lover? Could art withstand the allurements of Venice—Titian and Tintoretto, the cathedral of St. Mark and the Palace of the Doges, the birthplace of Desdemona and of Shylock, the home of Byron and of Browning?

She consented to a Roman marriage.

"I can't help wishing I could be a Papist just for that one day," she said lightly. "An Anglican marriage seems so dry and cold compared with the pomps and splendours of Rome."

"Dearest, the plainest Christian rites are enough, if they but make us one."

"I think we are that already, John," she answered shyly; and then, nestling by his side as they sat in the wide solitude of that stupendous pile, she took his hand and held it in both her own, looking down at it wonderingly—a well-formed hand, strong and muscular, broadened a little by seafaring.

"And you are to be my husband," she said. "Mine! I shall speak of you to people as my own peculiar property. 'My husband will do this or that.' 'My husband has gone out, but he will be home soon.' Home. Husband. How strange it sounds!"

"Strange and wonderful now, love. Sweet and familiar before our honeymoon is ended."

They went out of the broad spaces that were once populous with the teeming life of Imperial Rome, splendid with all that art could create of beauty and of grandeur—wrapt in the glamour of their dream. They walked all the way to the Piazza di Spagna in the same happy dream, as unconscious of the ground they trod on as if they had been floating in the air.

They were a very cheerful party at dinner that

evening. Father Rodwell dined with them, and was delighted at the idea of having to marry these happy lovers. He took the arrangement of the ceremony into his own hands. The English chaplain was his old friend, and would let him do what he liked in his church.

"It is to be a very quiet wedding," said the colonel, when the three men were smoking together in a loggia, looking on the little garden of orange trees and oleanders, in the grey dim beginning of night, when the thin crescent moon was shining in a sky still faintly flushed with sunset. "Isa could not stand anything like bustle or excitement. Luckily we have no friends in Rome. There is no one belonging to us who could be aggrieved at not being invited."

"And there is no one except Lostwithiel on my side who has the slightest claim to be present," said Hulbert. "I am almost as well off as the Flying Dutchman in that respect. I am not troubled with relations. All the kinsfolk I have are distant, and I allow them to remain so. My dear Disney, so far as I am concerned, our wedding cannot be too quiet a business. It is the bride I want, mark you, not the fuss and flowers, wedding-breakfast, and bridesmaids. Let us be married at half-past ten, and drive from the church to the railway station in time for the noonday train. I have given up my dream of taking Allegra round Southern Italy to the Adriatic. We shall go to Florence first, and spend a few days in the galleries, and thence to Venice, where we will have the *Vendetta* brought to us, and anchored near the arsenal, ready to carry us away directly we are tired of the city of old memories."

Father Rodwell left them and went into the drawing-room, where Isola and her sister-in-law were sitting in the lamplight—Isola's hands occupied with that soft, fluffy knitting which seemed to exercise a soothing influence upon her nerves; Allegra leaning over the table idly sketching with a light and rapid pencil random reminiscences of the Baths, the Tomb, the grave-eyed oxen, with their great curving horns and ponderous foreheads.

The priest was interested in watching Isola this evening. He saw a marked change in the expression of her countenance, a change which was perceptible to him even in her voice and manner—a brightness which might mean a lightened heart, or which might mean religious exaltation.

"Has she told him?" he wondered, studying her from his place in the shadow as the lamp-light shone full upon her wasted features and hectic colouring. "Has she taken courage and confessed her sin to that loyal, loving husband, and is the burden lifted from her heart?"

No; he could not believe that she had lifted the veil from the sad secret of her past. Martin Disney's unclouded brow to-night was not that of a man who had lately learned that the wife he loved had betrayed him. There might be pardon—there might be peace between husband and wife after such a revelation; but there could not be the serenity which he had seen in Martin Disney's manner to his wife to-night. Such a thunder-clap must leave its mark upon the man who suffered it. No; her secret was still locked in her impenitent heart. Sorry—yes. She had drunk the cup of remorse in all its bitterness; but she knew not true penitence, the Christian's penitence, which means self-abasement and con-fession. And yet she seemed happier. There was a look of almost holy resignation upon the pale and placid brow, and in the too-lustrous eyes. Something had happened—some moral transformation which made her a new being.

Father Rodwell drew his chair nearer to her, and looked at her earnestly with his cordial, almost boyish smile. He was a remarkably young-looking man, a man upon whom long years of toil in the dark places of the earth had exercised no wasting or withering influence. He had loved his work too well ever to feel the pressure of the burdens he carried. His gospel had been always a cheerful gospel, and he had helped to lighten sorrows, never to make them heavier. He was deeply interested in Isola, and had been watchful of all her changes of mood since their conversation in the shadow of the old Roman wall. He had seen her impressed by the history and traditions of the church, moved by the pathos of holy lives, touched almost to tears by sacred pictures, and he saw in her character and disposition a natural bent towards piety, exactly that receptive temperament which moves holy women to lives of self-abnegation and heroic endeavour. He had lent her some of those books which he loved best and read most himself, and he had talked with her of religion, careful not to say too much or with too strong an emphasis, and never by any word alluding to her revelation of past guilt. He wanted to win her to perfect trustfulness in him, to teach her to lean upon him in her helplessness; until the hour should come when she would let him lead her to her husband, in the self-abasement of the penitent sinner.

He looked at her in the lamplight, and her eyes met his with a straighter outlook than he had seen in them for a long time. She looked actually happy, and that look of happiness in a face on which death has set its seal has always something which suggests a life beyond the grave.

"The excitement of this marriage question has brightened you wonderfully, Mrs. Disney," he said. "We shall have you in high health by the wedding-day."

"I am feeling better because I am so glad," Isola answered naively, putting her hand into Allegra's.

"I consider it positively insulting to me as a

sister," exclaimed Allegra, bending down to kiss the too-transparent hand—such a hand as she had seen in many a picture of dying saint in that city. "You are most unaffectionately rejoiced to get rid of me. I have evidently been a tyrannical nurse, and a dull companion, and you breathe more freely at the prospect of release."

"You have been all that is dear and good," Isola answered softly, "and I shall feel dreadfully lonely without you; but it won't be for long. And I shall be so comforted by the knowledge that nothing can come between you and your life's happiness."

The two men came in from the loggia, bringing with them the cool breath of night. Isola went to the piano and played one of those Adagios of Mozart's which came just within the limit of her modest powers, and which she played to perfection, all her soul in the long lingering phrases, the tender modulations, with their suggestions of shadowy cathedral aisles, and the smoke of incense in the deepening dusk of a vesper service. Those bits of Mozart, the slow movements from the Sonatas, an Agnus

Dei, or an Ave Maria from one of the Masses, satisfied Captain Hulbert's highest ideas of music. He desired nothing grander or more scientific. The new learning of the Wagnerian school had no charm for him.

"If you ask me about modern composers, I am for Verdi and Gounod," he said. "For gaiety and charm, give me Auber, Rossini, and Boildieu—for pathos, Weber—for everything, Mozart. There you have the whole of my musical education."

The question of settlements was opened seriously between Martin Disney and his future brother-in-law, early on the following morning. Hulbert wanted to settle all the money he had in the world upon Allegra.

"She is ever so much wiser than I am," he said. "So she had better be my treasurer. My property is all in stocks and shares. My grandfather was fond of stock-jobbing, and made some very lucky investments which he settled upon my mother, with strict injunctions that they should not be meddled with by her trustees. My share of her fortune comes to a little over nine hundred a year. I came into possession

of it when I came of age, and it is mine to
dispose of as I like, trusts expired, trustees
cleared off—in point of fact, both gone over to
the majority, poor old souls, after having had
many an anxious hour about those South
American railway bonds, and Suez Canal shares,
which turned up trumps after all. I've tele-.
graphed to the family lawyer for a schedule
of the property, and when that comes, just tie
it all up in as tight a knot as the law can tie,
and let it belong to Allegra and her children
after her. Consider me paid off."

Martin Disney laughed at the lover's im-
petuosity—and told him that he should be
allowed to bring so much and no more into
settlement. Allegra's income was less than
two hundred a year, a poor little income upon
which she had fancied herself rich, so modest
is woman's measure of independence as compared with man's. It would be for the lawyer
to decide what proportion the husband's settle-·
ments should bear to the wife's income. Father
Rodwell had given Colonel Disney an intro-
duction to a solicitor of high character, a man
who had occupied an excellent position in

London until damaged lungs obliged him to seek a home in the south.

With this gentleman's aid, matters were soon put in train, and while the men were in the lawyer's office, the two women were choosing Allegra's wedding-gown.

The young lady had exhibited a rare indifference upon the great trousseau question. She was not one of those girls whose finery is all external, and who hide rags and tatters under æsthetic colouring and Watteau pleats. She was too much of an artist to endure anything unseemly in her belongings, and her everyday clothes, just as they were, might have been exhibited, like a Royal trousseau, without causing any other comment than, "How nice!" "What good taste!" "What exquisite needlework!"

The hands which painted such clever pictures were as skilful with the needle as with the brush, and Allegra had never considered that a vocation for art meant uselessness in every feminine industry. She had attended to her own wardrobe from the time she learnt plain sewing at her first school; and now, as she and Isola looked over the ample array of underlinen, the pretty cambric peignoirs, and neatly trimmed petticoats, they were both of one mind, that there was very little need of fuss or expenditure.

"I have plenty of summer frocks," said Allegra. "So really there is only my travelling gown to see about, that is to say, the gown I am to be married in."

"But you must have a real wedding-gown, all the same, a white satin gown, with lace and pearls," pleaded Isola. "When you go to dinner-parties, by-and-by, you will be expected to look like a bride."

"Dinner-parties! Oh, those are a long way off. We are not likely to be asked to any parties while we are wandering about Italy. I can get a gown when I go home."

Allegra's wedding-day had dawned—a glorious day—a day to make one drunken with the beauty of sky and earth; a day when the vetturini in the Piazza di Spagna sat and dreamt on their coach-boxes—narcotized by the sun— when the reds and blues in the garments of the flower-women were almost too dazzling for the eye to look upon, and when every garden in the city sent forth tropical odours of roses steeped in sunlight.

The church in which the lovers were to be made one was a very homely temple as compared with the basilicas yonder on the hills of Rome. But what did that matter to Allegra this morning as she stood before the altar and spoke the words which gave her to the man she loved? A flood of sunshine streamed upon the two figures of bride and bridegroom, and touched the almost spectral face of the bride's sister-in-law, a face which attracted as much attention as the bride's fresh bloom and happy smile. It was a face marked for death, yet beautiful in decay. The large violet eyes were luminous with the light that never was on land or sea—the light of worlds beyond the world we know. There was something loftier than happiness in that vivid look, something akin to exaltation—the smile of the martyr at the stake—the martyr for whom Heaven's miraculous intervention changes the flames of the death-pile into the soft fanning of seraphic wings; the martyr unconscious of earthly pains and earthly cruelties; who sees the

skies opening and the glorious company of saints
and angels gathered about the great white
throne.

Father Rodwell saw that spiritual expression
in the pale, wasted face, and he told himself that
a lost soul could not look out of eyes like those.
If death were near, as he feared, the true repentance for which he had prayed many an earnest
prayer was not far off.

Bride and bridegroom were to leave Rome by
the mid-day train. Colonel Disney was going to
see the last of them at the station, but Isola and
her sister-in-law were to say good-bye in the
vestry, and to part at the church door. And now
Father Rodwell's brief, but fervent, address had
been spoken, the Wedding March pealed from
the organ, and the small wedding-party went
into the vestry to sign the registers.

Isola was called upon for her signature as one
of the witnesses. She signed in a bold, clear
hand, without one tremulous line, her husband
looking over her shoulder as she wrote.

"That doesn't look like an invalid's autograph,
does it, Hulbert?" he asked, snatching at every

token of hope, unwilling to believe what his doctors and his own convictions told him— expecting a miracle.

They had warned him that he could not keep her long. They had advised him to humour her fancies, to let her be present at the wedding, even at the hazard of her suffering afterwards for that exertion and excitement. She would suffer more perhaps—physically as well as mentally—if she were thwarted in her natural wish to be by Allegra's side on that day.

All was finished. Neither Church nor law could do anything more towards making the lovers man and wife. The law might undo the bond for them in the time to come, but the part of the Church was done for ever. In the eye of the Church their union was indissoluble.

Isola clung with her arms round the bride's neck.

" Think of me sometimes, dearest, in the years to come. Think that I loved you fondly. Be sure that I was grateful for all your goodness to me," she said tearfully.

" My own love, I shall think of you every day till we meet again."

"And if we never meet again on earth—will you remember me kindly?"

"Isa, how can you?" cried Allegra, silencing the pale lips with kisses.

"You may be glad to think how much you did towards making my life happy—happier than it ought to have been." Isola went on in a low voice. "Dearest, I am more glad of your marriage than words can say; and, Allegra, love him with all your heart, and never let your lives be parted—remember, dearest, never, never let anything upon this earth part you from him."

Her voice was choked with sobs, and then came a worse fit of coughing than she had suffered for some time; a fit which left her exhausted and speechless. Her husband looked at her in an agony of apprehension.

"Let me take you home, Isa," he said. "You'll be better at home, lying down by your sunny window. This vestry is horribly cold. Hulbert, if you and Allegra will excuse me, I won't see you off at the station. Father Rodwell will go with you, perhaps. He'll be of more use than I could be; and we shall see each other very soon again in Switzerland, please God."

" Yes, yes. There is no need for you to go,"
Hulbert answered, grasping his hand, distressed
for another man's pain in the midst of his own
happiness. There death, and the end of all joy
—here the new life with its promises of gladness
just opening before him. Such contrasts must
needs seem hard.

They all went to the church door, where the
carriages were waiting. Only a few idlers
loitered about the pavement, faintly interested
in so shabby a wedding—a poor array of one
landau and one brougham, the brougham to take
the travellers to the station, where their luggage
had been sent by another conveyance.

The two women kissed each other once more
before Allegra stepped into the carriage, Isola
too weak for speech, and able only to clasp
the hands that had waited on her in so many
a weary hour; the clever hands, the gentle
hands, to which womanly instinct and womanly
love had given all the skilfulness of a trained
nurse.

Disney lifted his wife into the landau, Father
Rodwell helping him, full of sympathy.

" You'll dine with us to-night, I hope," said the

colonel. "We shall be very low if we are left to ourselves."

"I've an engagement for this evening—but— yes, I'll get myself excused, and spend the evening with you, if you really want me."

"Indeed we do," answered Disney, heartily ; but Isola was dumb. Her eyes were fixed upon the distant point at which the brougham had disappeared round a corner, on its way to the station.

CHAPTER XIV.

"GONE DEEPER THAN ALL PLUMMETS SOUND."

CHURCH bells are always ringing in that city of many churches, and there were bells ringing solemnly and slowly as Isola walked feebly up the two flights of stairs that led to Colonel Disney's lodging. She walked even more slowly than usual, and her husband could hear her labouring breath as she went up, step by step, leaning on the banister rail. He had offered her his arm, but she had repulsed him, almost rudely, at the bottom of the stairs.

They went into the drawing-room, which was bright with flowers in a sunlit dusk, the sun streaming in through the narrow opening between the Venetian shutters, which had been drawn together, but not fastened. All was very still in the quiet house; so still that they could hear the

splash of the fountain in the Piazza, and the faint
rustling of the limes in the garden.

Husband and wife stood facing each other, he
anxious and alarmed, she deadly pale, and with
gleaming eyes.

"Well, she is gone—she is Mrs. Hulbert now,
and she belongs to him and not to us any
more," said Disney, talking at random, watching his wife's face in nervous apprehension of
—he knew not what. "We shall miss her
sadly. Aren't you sorry she is married, Isola,
after all?"

"Sorry! No! I am glad—glad with all my
heart. I have waited for that."

And then, before he was aware, she had flung
herself at his feet, and was kneeling there, with
her head hanging down, her hands clasped—a
very Magdalen.

"I waited—till they were married—so that
you should not refuse to let her marry—his
brother—waited to tell you what I ought to have
told you at once, when you came home from
India. My only hope of pardon or of peace was
to have told you then—to have left you for ever
then—never to have dared to clasp your hand

—never to have dared to call myself your wife —never to have become the mother of your child. All my life since that day has been one long lie; and nothing that I have suffered—not all my agonies of remorse—can atone for that lie, unless God and you will accept my confession and my atonement to-day."

"Isola, for God's sake, stop!"

Again the racking cough seized her, and she sank speechless at his feet.

He lifted her in his arms and carried her to the sofa, and flung open the shutters and let the light and air stream in upon her, as she lay prostrate and exhausted, wiping her white lips with a blood-stained handkerchief. He looked at her in a kind of horrified compassion. He thought that she was raving, that the excitement of the morning had culminated in fever and delirium. He was going to ring for help, meaning to send instantly for her doctor, when she stopped him, laying her thin cold hand upon his arm, and holding him by her side.

"Sit down by me, Martin—don't stop me—I must tell you—all—the truth."

Her words came slowly, in gasps; then with

a great effort she gathered up the poor remnant of her strength, and went on in a low, tremulous voice, yet with the tone of one whose resolve was strong as death itself.

"There was a time when I thought I could never tell you—that I must go down to my grave with my sin unrevealed, and that you woul never know how worthless a woman you had loved and cherished. Then, on my knees before my God, I vowed that I would tell you all, at the last, when I was dying—and death is not far off now, Martin. I have delayed too long—too long! There is scarcely any atonement in my confession now. I have cheated you out of your love."

He looked at her horror-stricken, their two faces close to each other as he bent over her pillow.

No; this was no delirium—there was a terrible reality in her words. The eyes looking up at him were not bright with fever, but with the steady resolute soul within—the soul panting for freedom from sin.

"You have cheated me out of my love," he repeated slowly. "Does that mean that you lied to me that night in London—that you perjured yourself, calling God to witness that you were pure and true?"

"I was true to you then, Martin. My sin had been repented of. I was your loving, loyal wife, without one thought but of you."

"Loving, loyal!" he cried, with passionate scorn. "You had deceived and dishonoured me —you had made your name a by-word—a jest for such a man as Vansittart Crowther—and for how many more? You had lied, and lied, and lied to me—by every look, by every word that made you seem a virtuous woman and a faithful wife. My God, what misery!"

"Martin, have pity!"

"Pity! Yes, I pity the women in the streets! Am I to pity you, as I pity them? You, whom I worshipped—whom I thought as pure as the angels—wearing nothing of earth but your frail loveliness, which to me always seemed more of spirit than of clay. And you were false all the time—false as hell—the toy of the first idle profligate whom chance flung into your path? It was Lostwithiel! That man was right. He would hardly have dared to talk to you as he did it he had not been certain of his facts. Lostwithiel was your lover."

"Martin, have pity!" she repeated, with her hands clasped before her face.

"Pity! Don't I tell you that I pity you— pity you whom I used to revere! Great God! can you guess what pain it is to change respect for the creature one loves into pity? I told you that I would never hurt you—that I would never bring shame upon you, Isola. You have no unkindness to fear from me. But you have broken my heart, you have slain my faith in man and woman. I could have staked my life on your purity—I could have killed the man who slandered you—and you swore a false oath—you called upon Heaven to witness a lie!"

"I was a miserable, guilty creature, Martin. I could not bear to lose your love. If death had been my only penalty I could have borne it, but not the loss of your love."

"And your sister and her husband? They were as ready with their lies as you were," he exclaimed bitterly.

"Don't blame Gwendoline. I telegraphed to

her, imploring her to stand by me—to say that I was in London with her."

"And you were not in London?"

"No, except to pass through, when—when I had escaped from him, and was on my way home."

"Escaped! My God! What villainy must have been used against you—so young, so help-less! Tell me all—without reserve—as freely as you want to be forgiven."

"I was not utterly wicked, Martin. I did not sin deliberately—I did not know what I was doing when I wrecked my life and destroyed my peace of mind for ever. I never meant to forget you—or to be false to you—but I was so lonely —so lonely. The days were so dreary and so long—even the short autumn days seemed long —and the evenings were so melancholy without you. And he came into my life suddenly—like a prince in a fairy tale—and at first I thought very little about him. He was nothing more to me than any one else in Trelasco—and then somehow we were always meeting by accident— in the lanes—or by the sea—and he seemed to care for all the things I cared for. The books I loved were his favourites. For a long time we talked of nothing but his travels, and of my favourite books. There was not a word spoken between us that you or any one else could blame."

"'A common opening,' said Martin Disney, with scathing contempt. "One of the seducer's favourite leads."

"And then, one evening in the twilight, he told me that he loved me. I was very angry——and I let him see that I was angry, and I did all I could to avoid him after that evening. I refused to go to the ball at Lostwithiel, knowing that I must meet him there. But they all persuaded me—Mrs. Crowther, Mrs. Baynham, Tabitha—they were all bent upon making me go—and I went. Oh, God, if I had but stood firm against their foolish persuasion, if I had but been true to myself! But my own heart fought against me. I wanted to go to the ball—I wanted to see him again—if only for the last time. He had talked about starting for a long cruise to the Mediterranean. His yacht was ready to sail at an hour's notice."

"You went, and you were lost."

"Yes, it is all one long, wild dream when I look back upon it. He implored me to go away with him—but I told him no, no, no, not for worlds, nothing should ever make me false to my good, true husband—nothing. I swore it—swore an oath which I had not the strength to keep. Oh, it was cruel, heartless, treacherous —the thing he did after that. When I was going away from the dance, he was there at my side—and he put me into the wrong carriage— his own carriage—and when I had been driven a little way from the hotel, the carriage stopped and he got in. I thought that he was driving me home. I asked him how he could be so cruel as to be with me, in his own carriage, at the risk of my reputation—but he stopped me—shut my lips with his fatal kiss. Oh, Martin, how can I tell these things? The horse went almost at a gallop. I thought we should be killed. · I was half fainting when the carriage stopped at last, after rattling up and down hill—and he lifted me out, and I felt the cold night-air on my face, the salt spray from the sea. I tried to ask him where I was,—whether this was home—but the words died on my lips—and I knew no more

—knew no more till I woke from that dead, dull swoon in the cabin of the *Vendetta*, and heard the sailors calling out to each other, and saw Lostwithiel sitting by my side—and then—and then—it was all one long dream—a dream of days and nights, and rain, and tempest. I thought the boat was going down in that dreadful night in the Bay of Biscay. Would to God that she had gone down, and hidden me and my sin for ever! But she lived through the storm, and in the morning she was anchored near Arcachon, and Lostwithiel went on shore, and sent a woman in a boat, to bring me clothes, and to attend upon me; and I contrived to go on shore with the woman when she went back in the boat that had brought her, and I raised some money on my ring at a jeweller's in Arcachon, and I left by the first train for Paris, and went on from Paris to London, and never stopped to rest anywhere till I got home."

"May God bring me face to face with that ruffian who imposed upon your helplessness!" cried Martin Disney.

"No, no, Martin; he was not a ruffian. He betrayed me—but I loved him. He knew that

I loved him. I was as great a sinner as he. I was his before he stole me from my home—his in mind and in spirit. It was our unhappy fate to love each other. And I forgave him, Martin. I forgave him on that night of tempest, when I thought we were going to die together."

"You don't expect me to forgive him, do you? You don't expect me to forgive the seducer who has ruined your life and mine?"

"His brother is your sister's husband, Martin?"

"I am sorry for it."

"Oh, Jack Hulbert is good; he is frank and true. He is not like the other. But oh, Martin, pity Lostwithiel and his sin, as you pity me and my sin! It is past and done. I was mad when I cared for him—a creature under a spell. You won my heart back to you by your goodness —you made me more than ever your own. All that he had ever been to me—all that I had ever thought or felt about him—was blotted out as if I had never seen his face. Nothing remained but my love for you—and my guilty conscience, the aching misery of knowing that I was un-worthy of you."

He took her hand and pressed it gently in

silence. Then, after a long pause, when she had dried the tears from her streaming eyes, and was lying faint, and white, and still, caring very little what became of her poor remnant of life, he said softly—

"I forgive you, Isola, as I pray God to forgive you. I have spent some happy years with you— not knowing. If it was a delusion, it was very sweet—while it lasted."

"It was not a delusion," she cried, putting her arms round his neck, in a sudden rapture at being pardoned. "My love was real."

The door opened softly, and the kindly face of the Anglican priest looked in.

"I have seen the lovers on their way to Florence," he said, "and have come to ask how Mrs. Disney is after her fatiguing morning."

"I am happier than I have been for a long time," answered Isola, holding out her hand to him. "I am prepared for the end, let it come when it may."

He knew what she meant, and that the sinner had confessed her sin.

"Come out for a stroll with me, Disney," he said, "and leave your wife to rest for a little while. I'm afraid she'll miss her kind nurse."

Disney started up confusedly, like a sleeper awakened, and looked at his watch.

"I believe I have a substitute ready to replace Allegra by this time," he said, ringing the bell.

"Has the person from England arrived?" he asked the servant.

"Yes, sir. She came a quarter of an hour ago."

"Ask her to come here at once."

"Oh, Martin, you have not sent for a hospital nurse, I hope," cried Isola, excitedly. "Indeed I am not so bad as that. I want very little help. I could not bear to have a stranger about me."

"This is not a stranger, Isola."

There came a modest knock at the door as he spoke.

"Come in," he said; and a familiar figure in a grey merino gown and smart white cap with pink ribbons entered quietly and came to the sofa where Isola was lying.

"Tabitha!" she cried.

"Don't say you're sorry to see an old face again, Mrs. Disney. I told Mr. Martin that if you should ever be ill and want nursing I'd come to nurse you—if you were at the other end of the world—and Mr. Martin wrote and told me you wanted an old servant's care and experience to get you over your illness—and here I am. I've come every inch of the way without stopping, except at the buffets, and all I can say is Rome is a long way from everywhere, and the country I've come through isn't to be compared with Cornwall."

She ran on breathlessly as she seated herself by that reclining figure with the waxen face. It may be that she talked to hide the shock she had experienced on seeing the altered looks of the young mistress whose roof she had left in the hour of shame. She had left her, refusing to hold commune with one who had wronged the best of husbands. The faithful servant had taken leave of her mistress in words that had eaten into Isola's heart, as if they had been written there with a corrosive acid.

"I am very sorry for you, Mrs. Disney," she said. "You are young and pretty, and you are very much to be pitied—and God knows I have loved you as if you were my own flesh and blood.

But I won’t stay under the roof of a wife who has brought shame upon herself and has dishonoured the best of husbands.”

Isola had denied nothing, had acknowledged nothing, and had let Tabitha go. And now they met again for the first time after that miserable parting, and the servant’s eyes were full of pitying tears, and the servant’s lips spoke only gentlest words. What a virtue there must be in death, when so much is forgiven to the dying!

Martin Disney went out with the priest, but at the corner of the Piazza he stopped abruptly.

“Isola’s coughing fit has upset me more than it has her,” he said; “I’m not fit company for any one, so I think I’ll go for a tramp somewhere, and meet you later at dinner, when I’ve recovered my spirits a little.”

“*A riverderci*,” said the priest, grasping his hand. “I felicitate you upon this day’s union; a happy one, or I am no judge of men and women.”

“I don’t know,” Disney answered gloomily. “The woman is true as steel—the man comes of a bad stock. You know what the Scripture says about the tree and the fruit.”

"There never was a race yet that was altogether bad," said the priest. "Virtues may descend from remote ancestors as well as vices, —I think you told me moreover that Captain Hulbert's mother was a good woman."

"She was. She was one of my mother's earliest and dearest friends."

"Then you should have a better opinion of her son. If ever I met a thoroughly good fellow in my life, I believe I met one the day I made Captain Hulbert's acquaintance."

"Pray God you may be right," said Disney, with a sigh. "I am no judge of character."

He turned abruptly, and skirted the hill on his way to the gardens of the Villa Borghese, where he found shade and seclusion in the early afternoon. The carriages of fashionable Rome had not yet begun to drive in at the gate. The cypress avenues, the groves of immemorial ilex, the verdant lawns where the fountains leapt sunward, were peopled only by creatures of fable, fixed in marble, faun and dryad, hero and god. Martin Disney plunged into the shadow of one of those funereal avenues, and—while the sun blazed in almost tropical splendour upon the open lawn in the far distance—he walked as it were in the deep of night, a night whose gloom harmonized with that darker night in his despairing heart.

Great God, how he had loved her! How he had looked up to her, revering even her weakness as the expression of a child-like purity. And while he had been praying for her, and dreaming of her, and longing for her, and thinking of her as the very type of womanly chastity, unapproachable by temptation, unassailable, secure in her innocence and simplicity as Athene or Artemis with all their armour of defence; while he had so loved and trusted her, she had flung herself into the arms of a profligate—as easily won as the lightest wanton. She had done this thing, and then she had welcomed him with wan, sweet smiles to his dishonoured home; she had made him drink the cup of shame—a by-word it might be for the whole parish, as well as for that one man who had dared to hint at evil; and yet he had forgiven her—forgiven one to whom pardon meant only a peaceful ending; forgiven as a man holds himself forgiven by an all-merciful God, as he hears words of pity and promise murmured into his ear by the priest upon the scaffold, when the rope is round his neck and the drop is ready to fall. How could he withhold such pardon when he had been taught that God himself forgives the repentant murderer?

CHAPTER XV.

"THOUGH LOVE AND LIFE AND DEATH SHOULD COME AND GO."

ISOLA was alone in the spacious Roman drawing-room, its wide windows open to the soft, warm air. The sun was off that side of the house now, and the Venetian shutters had been pushed back; and between the heavy stone pillars of the loggia she saw the orange and magnolia trees in the garden, and the pale gold of the mimosas beyond. The sun was shining full upon the Hill of Gardens, that hill at whose foot Nero was buried in secret at dead of night by his faithful freedman and the devoted woman who loved him to the shameful end of the shameful life; that hill whose antique groves the wicked Cæsar's ghost had once made a place of terror. The wicked ghost was laid now. Modern civilization had sent Nero the way of all phantoms; and fashionable Rome made holiday on the Hill of Gardens. A military band was playing there this afternoon in the golden light, and the familiar melodies in Don Giovanni were wafted ever and anon in little gusts of sweetness to the loggia where the vivid crimson of waxen camelias and the softer rose of oleander blossoms gave brightness and colour to the dark foliage and the cold white stone.

Isola heard those far-off melodies faint in the distance — heard without heeding. The notes were beyond measure familiar, interwoven with the very fabric of her life, for those were the airs Martin Disney loved, and she had played them to him nearly every evening in their quiet, monotonous life. She heard, unheeding, for her thoughts had wandered back to the night of the ball at Lostwithiel and all that went after it— the fatal night that struck the death-knell of peace and innocence.

How vividly she remembered every detail— her fluttering apprehensions during the long drive in the dark lanes, up hill and down hill; her eagerness for the delight of the dance, as an unaccustomed pleasure—a scene to which young beauty flies as the moth to the flame; her remorseful consciousness that she had done wrong in yielding to the temptation which drew her there; the longing to see Lostwithiel once more — Lostwithiel, whom she had vowed to herself never to meet again of her own free will. She had gone home that afternoon resolved to forego the ball, to make any social sacrifice rather than look upon that man whose burning words of love, breathed in her ear before she had enough of nerve or calmness to silence him, had left her scathed and seared as if the lightning had blasted her. She had heard his avowal. There was no room now to doubt the meaning of all that had gone before, no ground now for believing in a tender, platonic admiration, lapping her round with its soft radiance—a light, but not a fire. That which had burnt into her soul to-day was the fierce flame of a dishonouring love, the bold avowal of a lover who wanted to steal her from her husband, and make her a sinner before her God.

She knew this much—had brooded upon it all the evening—and yet she was going to a place where she must inevitably meet the Tempter.

She was going because it was expedient to go; because her persistent refusal to be there might give rise to guesses and suspicions that would lead to a discovery of the real reason of her absence. She had often seen the subtle process, the society search-light by which Trelasco and Fowey could arrive at the innermost working of a neighbour's heart, the deepest mysteries of motive.

She was going to the ball after all, fevered, anxious, full of dim forebodings; and yet with an eager expectancy; and yet with a strange over-mastering joy. How should she meet him? How could she avoid him, without ostentatious avoidance, knowing how many eyes would be quick to mark any deviation from conventional behaviour? Somehow or other she was resolved to avoid all association with him; to get her programme filled before he could ask her to dance; or to refuse in any case if he asked her. He would scarcely venture to approach her after what had been said in the lane, when her indignation had been plainly expressed with angry tears.

No, he would hardly dare. And so—in a vague bewilderment at finding she was at her journey's end—she saw the lights of the little town close upon her, and in the next few minutes her carriage was moving slowly in the rank of carriages setting down their freight at the door of the inn.

Vaguely, as in a dream, she saw the lights and the flowers, the satin gowns and the diamonds, the scarlet and white upon the walls, brush and vizard, vizard and brush. He was not there. She looked along the crowd, and that tall figure and that dark head were absent. She ought to have been glad at this respite, and yet her heart grew heavy as lead.

Later he was there, and she was waltzing with him. At the last moment when he was standing before her, cool, self-possessed, as it were unconscious of that burning past, she had no more power to refuse to be his partner than the bird has to escape from the snake. She had given him her hand, and they were moving slowly, softly to the music of the soft, slow waltz. Myosotis, myosotis—mystic flower which means everlasting remembrance! Would she ever forget this night? Their last meeting—safest possible meeting-place here in the shine of the lamps—in the sight of the multitude. Here she could so easily hold him at bay. Here she might speak to him lightly, as if she too were unconscious of the past. Here she was safe against his madness and her own weak unstable heart, which fluttered at his smallest word.

And so the night wore on, and she danced with him more times than she could count, forgetting, or pretending to forget, other engagements; going through an occasional waltz with another partner just for propriety's sake, and hardly knowing who that partner was; knowing so well that there was some one else standing against the wall, watching her every movement with the love-light in his eyes.

Then came the period after supper when they sat in the ante-room and let the dances go by, hearing the music of waltzes which they were to have danced together, hearing and heeding not. And then came a sudden scare at the thought of the hour. Was it late?

Late, very late !

The discovery fluttered and unnerved her, and

she was scarcely able to collect her thoughts as he handed her into the carriage and shut the door.

"Surely it was a grey horse that brought me!" she exclaimed, and in the next minute she recognized Lostwithiel's brougham, the same carriage in which she had been driven home through the rain upon that unforgotten night when his house sheltered her, when she saw his face for the first time.

Yes, it was his carriage. She knew the colour of the lining, the little brass clock, the reading-lamp, the black panther rug. She pulled at the check-string, but without effect. The carriage drove on, slowly, but steadily, to the end of the town. She let down the window and called to the coachman. There was only one man on the box, and he took no notice of her call.

Yes, he had heard, perhaps, for he drew up his horse suddenly by the road-side, a little way beyond the town. A man opened the door and sprang in, breathless after running. It was Lostwithiel.

"You put me into your carriage!" she cried

distractedly. "How could you make such a mistake? Pray tell him to go back to the inn directly."

They were driving along the country road at a rapid pace, and he had seated himself by her side, clasping her hand. He pulled up the window nearest her, and prevented her calling to the coachman.

"Why should you go back? You will be home sooner with my horse than with the screw that brought you."

"But the fly will be waiting for me—the man will wonder."

"Let him wonder. He won't wait very long, you may be assured. He will guess what has happened. In the confusion of carriages you took the wrong one. Isola, I am going to leave Cornwall to-night—to leave England—perhaps never to return. Give me the last few moments of my life here. Be merciful to me. I am going away—perhaps for ever."

"Take me home," she said. "Are you really taking me home? Is this the right way?"

"Of course it is the right way. Do you suppose I am going to drive you to London?"

He let down the glass suddenly, and pointed into the night.

"Isola, do you see where we are? There's the sign-post at the cross roads. There's the tower of Tywardreath Church, though you can hardly see it in this dim light. Are you satisfied now?"

He had drawn up the glass again. The windows were growing dim with the mist of their mingled breath; the atmosphere was faint with the odour of the faded chrysanthemums on her gown and the carnation in the lapel of his coat. All that she could see of the outer world was the blurred light of the carriage lamps. The high-spirited horse was going up and down the hills at a perilous pace. At this rate the journey could not take long.

And then—and then—he came back to the prayer he had breathed in her ear more than twelve hours ago in the wintry lane. He loved her, he loved her, he loved her! Could she refuse to go away with him—having woven herself into his life, having made him madly, helplessly in love with her? Could she refuse? Had any woman the right to refuse? He appealed to her sense of honour. She had gone too far—she had granted too much already, granting him her love. She was in his arms in the dim light, in the faint, dream-like atmosphere. He was taking possession of her weak heart by all that science of love in which he was past master. Honour, conscience, fidelity to the absent, piety, innocence were being swept away in that lava flood of passion. Helpless, irresolute, she faltered again and again. "Take me home, Lostwithiel! Have mercy! Take me home."

He stopped those tremulous lips with a kiss— the kiss that betrays. The carriage dashed down a steep hill, rattled along a street so narrow that the wheels seemed to grind against the house-fronts on each side, down hill again, and then the horse was pulled up suddenly in a stony square, and the door opened, and the soft, sweet sea-breeze blew among her loosened hair, and upon her uncovered neck, and she heard the gentle plish-plash of a boat moored against the quay at her feet.

"This is not home!" she cried piteously.

"Yes, it is home, love, our home for a little

while—the home that can carry us to the other end of the world, if you will."

The quay, and the water, and the few faint lights here and there grew dark, and she knew no more, till she heard the sailors crying, "Yeo, heave, yeo," and the heavy sails flapping, and the creak of the boom as it swayed in the wind, and felt the dancing motion of the boat as she cut her way through the waves, felt the strong arm that clasped her, and heard the low, fond voice that murmured in her ear, "Isola, Isola, forgive me! I could not live without you."

That which came afterwards had seemed one long and lurid dream—a dream of fair weather and foul; of peril and despair; of passionate, all-conquering love.

To-day, as she lay supine in the afternoon silence—lying as Tabitha had left her, in a fevered sleep—the vision of that past came back upon her in all its vivid colouring, almost as distinctly as it had reacted itself in her hours of delirium, when she had lived that tragic chapter of her life over again, and had felt the fury of the waves and breathed the chill, salt air of the tempest-driven sea, and had seen the moon riding high amidst the cloud-chaos—now appearing, now vanishing, as if she too were a storm-driven bark in a raging sea.

Oh God! how vividly those hours came back! The awful progress from Ushant to Arcachon; the darkness of the brief day; the horror of the long night; the shuddering yacht, with straining spars, and broadside beaten by a heaving mass of water, that struck her with the force of a thousand battering-rams, blow after blow, each blow seeming as if the next must always be the last—the final crash and end of all things. The pretty, dainty vessel, long and narrow, rode like an eggshell on those furious waters—here a long wall of inky blackness, rising like a mountain-ridge, and bearing down on the doomed ship, and beyond, as far as the eye could reach, a waste of surf, livid in the moonlight. What helpless insignificance, as of a leaf tossed on a whirlpool, when that mountainous mass took the yacht and lifted her on cyclopean shoulders, and shook her off again into the black trough of the sea, as into the depths of hell! And this not once only, nor a hundred times only, but on through that endless-seeming night, on in the sickly winter dawn and in the faint yellow gleam of a rainy noontide—on through day that seemed mixed and entangled with night, as if the beginning of creation had come round again, and the light were not yet divided from the darkness.

Oh, those passionate, never-to-be-forgotten moments, when she had stood with him at the top of the companion, looking out upon those livid waters, over that sea of death; fondly believing that each moment was to be their last; that the gates of death were opening yonder— a watery way, a gulf to which they must go down, in a moment, in a little moment, in a flash, in a breath, at the next, or the next, or the next mad plunge of that hurrying bark. Yes, death was there, in front of them—inevitable, imminent, immediate—and life and sin, shame, remorse, were done with, along with the years that lay behind them, a page blotted and blurred with one passionate madness, which had changed the colour of a woman's life history. She knew not how she bore up against the force of that tempest; clinging to him with her bare, wet arms; held up by him; crouching against the woodwork, which shook and rattled with every blow of the battering-rams. She only knew that his arms were round her, that she was safe with him, even when the leaping surf rose high above her head, wrapping her round like a mantle, blinding, drowning her in a momentary extinction. She only knew that his lips were close to her ear, and that in an instant's lull of those awful voices he murmured, "We are going to die, Isola! The boat cannot live through such a storm! We shall go down to death together!" And her lips turned to him with a joyful cry, "Thank God!" Then again, in a momentary pause, he pleaded, "Forgive me, love; my stolen love, forgive me before we die!" And again, "Was it a crime, Isola?" "If it was, I forgive you!" she whispered, clinging to him as the blast struck them.

Cruel revulsion of feeling, bitter irony of Fate, when the great grim waves—which had seemed like living monsters hurrying down upon them with malignant fury to tear and to devour—when the awful sea began to roar with a lesser voice, and the thunder of the battering-rams had a duller sound, and the bows of the yacht no longer plunged straight down into the leaden-coloured pit; no longer climbed those inky ridges with such blind impetus, as of a cockle-shell in a whirlpool. Bitter sense of loss and dismay when the grey, cold dawn lighted a quieter sea, and she heard the captain telling Lostwithiel that they had seen the worst of the storm, and that there was no fear now. He was going to put on more canvas: and hadn't the lady better go below, where it was warm. She needn't feel anyway nervous now. They would soon be in the roadstead off Arcachon.

She had not felt the chill change from night to morning. She had not felt the surf that drenched her loose, entangled hair. She hardly knew when or how Lostwithiel had wrapped her in his fur-lined coat; but she found that she was so enveloped presently when she stumbled and staggered down to the cabin, and flung herself face downward upon the sofa, in a paroxysm of impotent despair.

Death would have delivered her. The tempest was her friend; and the tempest had passed her by, and left her lying there like a weed, more worthless than any weed that ever the sea cast up to rot upon the barren rocks. Yes, she was left there; left in a life that sin had blighted; loathsome to herself, hateful to her God.

She locked herself in the cabin, while the hurrying footsteps overhead told her that Lostwithiel was working with the sailors.

An hour later, and he was at the cabin door, pleading for one kind word, entreating her to let him see her, were it only for a few moments, to know that she was not utterly broken down by the peril she had passed through. He pleaded in vain. She would give no answer—she would speak no word. Indeed, in that dull agony of shame and despair it seemed to her as if a dumb devil had entered into her. Her parched lips seemed to have lost the power of speech. She lay there, staring straight before her at all the swinging things on the cedar panel—the books and photographs—and lamps and frivolities, swaying and vibrating with every movement of the sea. Her hands were clenched until the nails cut into the flesh. Her heart was throbbing with dull, slow beats that made themselves torturingly audible. Did God create his creatures for such agony? Had she been foredoomed ever-

lastingly—in that awful incomprehensible ante-
natal Eternity—foredoomed to this fallen state,
to this unutterable shame?

Hours went by, she knew not how. Again and
again Lostwithiel came to her door, and talked and
entreated—Heaven knows how tenderly—with
what deep contrition, with what fond pleading
for pardon. But the dumb devil held her still.
She wrapped herself in a sullen despair—not
anger, for anger is active. Hers was only a
supine resistance.

At last she heard him come with one of the
sailors, and she could make out from their
whispering talk that they were going to force
open the door. Then she started up in a kind of
fury, and went and flung herself against the
cedar panels.

"If you don't leave me alone in my misery I
will kill myself!" she cried.

The long night was over; and the sun was
high. It seemed as if they were sailing over a
summer sea, and through the scuttle port she saw
a little foreign town nestling under the shelter of
pine-clad hills.

She woke from brief and troubled slumbers to

see this smiling shore, and at first she fancied they must have sailed back to Cornwall, and that this was some unknown bay upon that rock-bound coast; but the sapphire sea and the summer-like sunshine suggested a fairer clime than rugged Britain.

While she was looking out at the crescent-shaped bay, and the long line of white villas, the anchor was being lowered. The sea was almost as smooth as a lake, and those tranquil waters had the colour and the sheen of sapphire and emerald. She thought of the jasper sea—the sea of the Apocalypse, the tideless sea beside that land of the New Jerusalem where there are no more tears, where there can be no more sin, a city of ransomed souls, redeemed from all earth's iniquity.

A boat was being lowered. She heard the scroop of the rope against the hull; she heard footsteps on the accommodation-ladder, and then the dip of oars, and presently the boat passed between her and the sunlit waters, and she saw Lostwithiel sitting in the stern, with the rudder-lines in his hands, while two sailors were bending to their oars, with wind-blown hair and cheery, smiling faces, broad and red in the gay morning sunshine.

He was gone, and she breathed more freely. There was a sense of release in his absence; and for the first time she looked round the cabin, where beautiful and luxurious things lay, thrown here and there in huddled masses of brilliant colour. A Japanese screen, a masterpiece of gold and rainbow embroidery on a sea-green ground, flung against the panelling at one end—chairs, vases, wicker-work tables overturned—Persian curtains wrenched from their fastenings and hanging awry—satin pillows that had drifted into a heap in one corner—signs of havoc everywhere. She stood in the midst of all this ruin, and looked at her own reflection in a long Venetian glass fastened to the panelling, about the only object that had held its place through the storm.

Her own reflection. Was that really herself, that ghastly image which the glass gave back to her? The reflection of a woman with livid cheeks and blanched lips, with swollen eyelids, and dark rings of purple round the haggard eyes, and hair rough and tangled as Medusa's locks, and bare shoulders from which the stained satin bodice had slipped away. Her wedding-gown! Could that defiled garment—the long folds of the once shining satin, draggled and befouled with the tar from the cordage and the spray from the sea, heavy and dripping with sea-water—could these tawdry rags be the wedding-gown she had put on in her proud and happy innocence in the old bedroom at Dinan, with mother, and servants, and a useful friend or two helping and hindering?

Oh, if they could see her now, those old friends of her unclouded childhood, the mother and father who had loved and trusted her, who had never spoken of evil things in her hearing, had never thought that sin could come near her! And she had fallen like the lowest of womankind. She had forfeited her place among the virtuous and happy for ever. She, Martin Disney's wife! That good man, that brave soldier who had fought for Queen and country—it was his wife who stood there in her shame, haggard and dishevelled!

She flung her arms above her head and wrung her hands in a paroxysm of despair. Then, with

a little cry, she plucked at the loose wild tresses
as if she would have torn them from her head;
and then she threw herself upon the cabin floor
in her agony, and grovelled there, a creature for
whom death would have been a merciful release.

"If I could die—if I could but die, and no
one know!" she moaned.

She lifted herself up again upon her knees,
and, with one hand upon the floor, looked round
the walls of the cabin—looked among all that
glittering array of yataghans and barbaric shields,
damascened steel and jewelled hilts, for some
practical instrument with which she might take
her hated life.   And then came the thought of
what must follow death, not for her in the dim
incomprehensible eternity, but for those who
loved her on earth, for those who would have
to be told how she had been found, in her
draggled wedding-gown, stabbed by her own
hand on board Lord Lostwithiel's yacht.   What
a story of shame and crime for newspapers to
embellish, and for scandal-lovers to gloat over!
No! She dared not destroy herself thus. She
must collect her senses, escape from her seducer,
and keep the secret of her dishonour.

She took off her gown, and rolled train and bodice into a bundle as small as she could make them. Then she looked about the cabin for some object with which to weight her bundle. Yes, that would do. A little brass dolphin that was used to steady the open door. That was heavy enough perhaps. She put it into the middle of her bundle, tied a ribbon tightly round the whole, and then she opened the scuttle port and dropped her wedding-garment into the sea. The keen winter wind, the wind from pine-clad hills and distant snow mountains, blew in upon her bare neck and chilled her to the bone; but it helped to cool the fever of her mind, and she sat down and leant her head upon her clasped hands, and tried to think what she must do to escape from the toils in which guilty love had caught her.

She must escape from the yacht. She must go back to England—somehow.

She thought that if she were to appeal to Lostwithiel's honour some spark of better feeling would prevail over that madness which had wrecked her, and he would let her go, he would take her back to England, and facilitate her secret return to the home she had dishonoured. But could she trust herself to make that appeal? Could she stand fast against his pleading, if he implored her to stay with him, to live the life that he had planned for her, the life that he had painted so eloquently, the dreamy, beautiful life amidst earth's most poetic scenes, the life of love in idleness? Could she resist him if he should plead—it might be with tears—he, whom she adored, her destroyer and her divinity? No, she must leave the yacht before he came back to her. But how?

There were only men on board. There was no woman to whose compassion she could appeal, no woman to lend her clothes to cover her. She saw herself once again in the Venetian glass, in her long trained petticoat of muslin and lace, so daintily fresh when she dressed for the ball— muslin and lace soddened by the sea, torn to shreds where her feet had caught in the dainty flouncings as she stumbled down the companion during last night's storm. A fitting costume in which to travel from Arcachon to London, verily! She opened a door leading to an inner cabin, which contained bed and bath, and all toilet appliances. Hanging against the wall there were three dressing-gowns, the lightest and least masculine of the three being a robe of Indian camel's hair, embroidered with dull, brown silk —a neutral tinted shapeless garment with loose sleeves and a girdle.

Here, within locked doors, she made her hurried toilet, with much cold water. She brushed her long, ragged hair with one of the humblest of the brushes. She would not take so much as a few drops from the great crystal bottle of eau de Cologne which was held in a silver frame suspended from the ceiling. Nothing of his would she touch, nothing belonging to the man who wanted to pour his fortune into her lap, to make his life her life, his estate her estate, his name her name, could she but survive the ordeal of the divorce court, and shake off old ties.

She rolled her hair in a large coil at the back of her head. She put on the camel's hair dressing-gown, and tied the girdle round her long, slim waist, and having done this she looked altogether a different creature from that vision of haggard shame which she had seen just now with loathing. She had a curious puritan air in her sad coloured raiment, and braided hair.

Scarcely had she finished when she heard the dip of oars, and looking out in an agony of horror at the apprehension of Lostwithiel's return, she saw a boat laden with two big milliner's baskets, and with a woman sitting in the stern. The men who were rowing this boat were not of the crew of the *Vendetta.*

She had not long to wonder. She unlocked her door, and went into the adjoining cabin, while the boat came alongside, and woman and baskets were hauled upon the deck.

Three minutes afterwards the cabin-boy knocked at her door, and told her that there was a person from Arcachon to see her, a dressmaker with things that had been ordered for her.

She unlocked the door, for the first time since she locked it last night, and found herself face to face with a smiling young person, whose black eyes and olive complexion were warm with the glow of the south, golden in the eyes, carnation on the plump, oval cheeks.

This young person had the honour to bring

the trousseau which Monsieur had sent for
Madame's inspection. Monsieur had told her
how sadly inconvenienced Madame had been
by the accident by which all her luggage had
been left upon the quay at the moment of
sailing. In truth it must have been distressing
for Madame, as it had evidently been distressing
for Monsieur in his profound sympathy with
Madame, his wife. In the meantime she, the
young person, had complied with Monsieur's
orders, and had brought all that there was of
the best and most delicate and refined for
Madame's gracious inspection.

The cabin-boy brought in the two baskets,
which the milliner opened with an air, taking
out the delicate lingerie, the soft silk and
softer cashmere—peignoirs, frilled petticoats,
a fluff and flutter of creamy lace and pale satin
ribbons, transforming simplest garments into
things of beauty. She spread out her wares,
chattering all the while, and then looked at
Madame for approval.

Isola scarcely glanced at all the finery. She
pointed to the only plain walking-gown among
all the delicate prettinesses, the silks and cash-

meres and laces—a grey tweed, tailor-gown, with no adornment except a little narrow black braid.

"I will keep that," she said, " and one set of underlinen, the plainest. You can take all the rest of the things back to your shop. Please help me to dress as quickly as you can—I want to go on shore in the boat that takes you back."

" But, Madame, Monsieur insisted that I should bring a complete trousseau. He wished Madame to supply herself with all things needful for a long cruise in the south."

"He was mistaken. My luggage is safe enough. I shall have it again in a few days. I only want clothes to wear for a day or two. Kindly do what I ask."

Her tone was so authoritative that the milliner complied, reluctantly, and murmuring persuasive little speeches while she assisted Madame to dress. All that she had brought was of the most new—expressly arrived from Paris, from one of the most distinguished establishments in the Rue de la Paix. Fashions change so quickly— and the present fashions were so enchanting, so original. She must be pardoned if she suggested that nothing in Madame's wardrobe could be so new or so elegant as these last triumphs of an artistic faiseur. Madame took no heed of her eloquence, but hurried through the simple toilet, insisted upon all the finery being replaced in the two baskets, and then went upon deck with the milliner.

"I am going on shore to his lordship," she said, with quiet authority, to the captain.

It was a deliberate lie—the first she had told, but not the last she would have to tell.

She landed on the beach at Arcachon—penni-less, but with a diamond ring on her wedding finger—her engagement ring—which she knew, by a careless admission of Martin Disney's, to have cost fifty pounds. She left the milliner, and went into the little town, dreading to meet Lostwithiel at every step. She found a com-placent jeweller who was willing to advance twenty-five Napoleons upon the ring, and promised to return it to her on the receipt of that sum, with only a bagatelle of twenty francs for interest, since Madame would redeem her pledge almost immediately.

Furnished with this money she drove straight

to the station, and waited there in the most obscure corner she could find till the first train left for Bordeaux. At Bordeaux she had a long time to wait, still in hiding, before the express left for Paris—and then came the long, lonely journey—from Bordeaux to Paris—from Paris to London—from London to Trelasco—it seemed an endless pilgrimage, a nightmare dream of dark night and wintry day, made hideous by the ceaseless throb of the engine, the perpetual odour of sulphur and smoke. She reached Trelasco somehow, and sank exhausted in Tabitha's arms.

"What day is it?" she asked faintly, looking round the familiar room, as if she had never seen it before.

"Thursday, ma'am. You have been away ten days," the old servant answered coldly.

It was only the next day that Tabitha told her mistress she must leave her.

"There is no need to talk about what has happened," she said. "I have kept your secret. I have let no one know that you were away. I packed Susan off for a holiday the morning after the ball. I don't believe any one knows anything about you—unless you were seen yesterday on your way home."

Then came stern words of renunciation, a conscientious but rather narrow-minded woman's protest against sin.

CHAPTER XVI.

"I, YOU, AND GOD CAN COMPREHEND EACH OTHER."

IT was two months after Allegra's wedding-day, and Martin Disney had been warned that the closing hour of the young life he had watched so tenderly was not far off. It might come to-morrow; or it might not come for a week; or the lingering flame might go flickering on, fainting and reviving in the socket, for another month. He must hold himself prepared for the worst. Death might come suddenly at the last, like a thief in the night; or by stealthy, gradual steps, and slowest progress from life to clay.

He sat beside Isola's sofa in the Roman lodging as he had sat beside her bed in that long illness at Trelasco, when her wandering mind appalled him more than her bodily weakness. He watched as faithfully as he had watched then, but this time without hope.

Father Rodwell had been with her at seven o'clock upon the last three mornings, and had administered the sacrament to her and to her husband, and to the faithful Tabitha, one with them in piety and love. The priest thought that each celebration would be the last; but she rallied a little as the day wore on, and lived till sunset; lived through the long painful night; and another day dawned, and he found her waiting for him in the morning, ready to greet him with her pale smile when he appeared upon the threshold of her room, after going up the staircase in saddest apprehension, dreading to hear that all was over, except the funeral service and the funeral bell.

She insisted upon getting up and going into the drawing-room, feeble as she was. Tabitha was so handy and so helpful that the fatigue of an invalid's toilet was lightened to the uttermost. Tabitha and the colonel carried her from the bedroom to the drawing-room upon her couch, and carried the couch back to the bedside in the evening. Before noon she was lying in the sunlit saloon, surrounded with flowers and photographs and books and newspapers, and all things that lighten the monotonous hours of sickness.

Nor was companionship ever wanting. Martin Disney devoted himself to her with an unfailing patience. Upon no pretence would he leave her for more than half an hour at a time—just the space of a walk to the Hill of Gardens, or the length of the Via de' Condotti and the Corso; just the space of a cigar in the loggia.

He read to her, he talked to her, he waited upon her. Tabitha and he were her only nurses; for Löttchen was a young woman of profound concentration of motive, and had early taken unto herself the motto, One baby, one nurse. She conscientiously performed her duty to her infant charge; but she rarely lifted a finger to help any one else.

It was drawing towards the end of July; the weather had been lovely hitherto—hot, and very hot, but not insupportable for those who could afford to dawdle and sleep away their mid-day and afternoon existence—who had horses to carry them about in the early mornings, and a carriage to drive them in moonlit gardens and picturesque places. In the suburbs of the great city, across the arid Campagna yonder, at Tivoli, and Frascati, and Albano, and Castel Gandolfo, people had been revelling in the fulness of the summer, living under Jove's broad roof, with dancing and sports, and music and feasting, and rustic, innocent kisses, snatched amidst the darkness of groves whose only lamps are fireflies—deep woods of ilex, where the nightingale sings long and late, and the grasshopper trills his good night through the perfumed herbage.

Here, in Rome, the heat was more oppressive, and the splashing of the city's many fountains was the only relief from the glare and dazzle of the piazzas, the vivid whiteness of the great blocks of houses in the new streets and boulevards. Blinds were lowered, and shops were shut, in the blinding noontide heat, and through the early afternoon the eternal city was almost as silent and reposeful as the sleeping beauty— to awaken at sundown to movement, and life, and music, and singing, in lighted streets and crowded cafés.

Suddenly, in the dim grey of the morning, the slumberous calm of summer changed to howling wind and tropical rain—torrential rain, that fell in sheets of water, and filled every gutter, and splashed from every housetop, and ran in wild cascades from every alley on the steep hillsides. The Campagna was one vast lake, illumined with vivid flashes of lightning, and the thunder pealed and reverberated along the lofty parapets of the ruined aqueducts. The tall cypresses in the Pincian Gardens bent like saplings before that mighty wind, which seemed to howl and shriek its loudest as it came tearing down from the hill to whistle and rave among the housetops in the Piazza di Spagna.

"One would think the ghost of Nero were shrieking in the midst of the tempest," said Isola, as she listened to the fitful sobbing of the wind late in the dull grey afternoon, while her husband and Father Rodwell sat near her couch, keeping up that sad pretence of cheerfulness which love struggles to maintain upon the very edge of the grave—the broken-hearted make-believe of those who know that death waits at the door. "There comes a shrill cry every now and then like the scream of a wicked spirit in pain."

" Rome is full of ghosts," answered the priest,

"but there are the shadows of the good and the great as well as of the wicked. Walking alone in twilight on the Aventine, I should hardly be surprised to meet the spirit of Gregory the Great wandering amidst the scenes of his saintly life; nor do I ever go into the Pantheon at dusk without half expecting to see the shade of Raffaelle. And there are others—some I knew in the flesh—Wiseman and Antonelli, Gibson, the sculptor, consummate artist and gentlest of men—yes, Rome is full of the shadows of the good and the wise. One can afford to put up with Nero."

"You don't mean me to think that you believe in ghosts?" asked Isola, deeply interested.

It was only five o'clock, yet the sky was grey with the greyness of late evening. Here in this land of light and sunshine there had been all day long the brooding gloom of storm-clouds, and a sky that was dark as winter.

"I won't analyze my own feelings on the subject; I will quote the words of a man at whose feet it was my happiness to sit sometimes when I was a lad at Oxford. Canon Mozley has not shrunk from facing the great problem of spiritual life in this world—of an invisible after-existence upon the earth when the body is dust. 'Is the mother of our Lord now existing?' he asks, and answers, 'Yes. I believe that all fathers, mothers, sons, and daughters are now existing. Nature has disposed of their bodies as far as we can trace her work; but their souls remain. So I read in Homer, in Virgil, and in the New Testament. This existence I am permitted to believe is a conscious and active existence.' Canon Mozley, the man who wrote those words and much more in the same strain, was not an idle visionary. If he could afford to believe in the presence of the dead among us, why so can I. And I believe that Gregory the Great has whispered at the ear of many a Holy Father in the long line of his successors, and has influenced many a Cardinal's vote, and has been an invisible power in many a council."

"I like to believe in ghosts," said Isola, gently. "But I thank God those that I love are still in this life."

She held out her hand with a curiously timid gesture to her husband, who clasped it tenderly, bending his lips to kiss the pale thin fingers. Oh, Death, pity and pardon are so interwoven with thine image that neither pride nor anger has any force against thy softening influence. She had been false. She had wronged him and dishonoured herself, cruelly, cruelly, most cruelly; but she had suffered and repented, and she was passing away from him. Let the broken spirit pass in peace!

"Hark!" she cried.

That day wore itself out in storm and tempest, and the night came on like a fierce death-struggle; and the wind raved and shrieked at intervals all through the night; and again next day there were gloom and darkness, and a sky heaped up with masses of lead-coloured cloud; and again the torrential rain streamed from the housetops and splashed in the streets below; a dreary day to be endured even by the healthy and the happy—a day of painful oppression for an invalid. Isola's spirits sank to the lowest depth, and for the first time since Allegra's marriage she talked hopelessly of their separation.

"If I could only see her once more before I die," she sighed.

"My dear love, you shall see her as soon as the railway can bring her here. Remember, it is you who have forbidden me to send for her. You know how dearly she loves you—how willingly she would come to you. I'll telegraph to her within half an hour."

"No, no, no," Isola protested hurriedly. "No, we can never meet again in this world. I took my farewell of her in the church. I meant it to be farewell. I was very happy for her sake when I saw her married to the man she loved. It was a selfish repining that made me ask for her just now. I would not have her summoned here for worlds. She is so happy at Venice—happy in her honeymoon dream. Tell her nothing, Martin—nothing till you can tell her that my days have ended peacefully. She has borne her burden for me in the past. I want her to be free from all care about me—but not to forget me."

"She will not forget, Isola. She loves you fondly and truly."

"Yes, I am sure of that. She was dearer to me than my own sister—cared for me much more than Gwendoline ever cared, though Gwen and

I were always good friends. Poor frivolous Gwen! She writes me affectionate letters, hoping she may get to Italy in the autumn, though it is impossible for her to come just now. And mother and father write to me just in the same way—mother regretting that her health won't allow her to leave Dinan; father hoping to see me in the autumn. Their letters are full of hopefulness," she concluded, with a faint touch of irony.

Her husband read to her for the greater part of the long gloomy day. He read St. Thomas à Kempis for some part of the time. The book had been on the little table by her side throughout her illness. He read two or three of Frederick Robertson's sermons, and for occasional respite from too serious thought he read her favourite poems—Adonaïs, Alastor, and some of Shelley's lovely lyrics, and those passages in Childe Harold which had acquired a new charm for her since she had grown familiar with Rome.

"Read to me about Venice," she said, "and let me think of Allegra and Captain Hulbert. I love to fancy them gliding along those narrow, picturesque streets, in the great, graceful, ponderous gondola I remember so well. It is so nice to know of their happiness—and to know that they need never be parted."

So the long summer day—without the glow and glory of summer—wore on, and except for her excessive languor and feebleness there were no indications that the patient's state was any worse than it had been for some weeks. The doctor came late in the afternoon, and felt her pulse, and talked to her a little; but it was easy to see that his visit was only a formula.

"You have such an excellent nurse, Mrs. Disney, that I consider my position almost a sinecure," he said, smiling at the faithful Tabitha, who stood waiting for his instructions, and who never forgot the minutest detail.

Tabitha came in from the adjoining bedroom every now and then, and adjusted the pillows on the sofa, and sprinkled eau de Cologne, or fanned the invalid with a large Japanese fan, or arranged the soft silken coverlet over her feet, or brought her some small refreshment in the way of a cup of soup or jelly, and tenderly coaxed and assisted her to take it, talking just as much or as little

as seemed prudent, always careful neither to
fatigue nor excite her charge.

It was between eight and nine in the evening,
and there was a gloomy twilight in the loggia,
and in the garden beyond. The wind which had
dropped in the afternoon had begun to rage
again, as if not only Nero but all the wicked
emperors were abroad in the air.

Isola had begged that one of the windows
might be opened, in spite of the tempestuous
weather; and the cold damp breath of the storm
crept into the room and chilled Martin Disney
as he sat by his wife's sofa, reading a London
paper that had come by the evening post.

The only artificial light in the room was a
reading-lamp at the colonel's elbow, shaded from
the draught by the four-leaved screen which
protected the invalid. The gloomy grey daylight
had not quite faded, and through the half-open
door opposite him Martin Disney saw the white
marble wall of the staircase, and some oleanders
in stone vases that stood on the spacious landing.

He had been reading to Isola nearly all day.
He was reading to himself now, trying to forget

his own grief in the consideration of a leading article which prophecied a European war, and the ultimate extinction of English influence in continental politics.

There was perfect stillness in the room. Isola had been lying with closed eyes a little time before, and he fancied that she was sleeping.

The silence had lasted for nearly an hour, broken only by the shriek of the wind, and by the chiming of the quarters from the Church of La Trinita de' Monte, when Colonel Disney was startled by his wife's hand clutching his arm, and his wife's agitated whisper sounding close to his ear.

"Martin! Did you see him?"

She had lifted herself into a sitting position, she who had not been able to sit up for many days past.

The hectic bloom had faded from her cheeks and left them ashy pale. Her eyes seemed almost starting from her head, straining their gaze as if to penetrate the deepening shadows on the landing beyond the half-open door.

"My love, you have been dreaming," said Disney, soothing her with womanly gentleness. "Lie down again, my poor dear. See, let me arrange the pillows and make you quite comfortable."

"No, no! I was not dreaming. I have not been asleep. He was there; I saw him as plainly as I see you. He pushed the door a little further open and looked in at me. I saw his face in the lamplight, very pale."

Disney glanced at the door involuntarily. Yes, the aperture was certainly wider than when he looked at it last; just as if some one's hand had pushed the door further ajar. The hand of the wind no doubt.

"My dear girl, believe me, you were dreaming. No one could have approached that doorway without my hearing them."

"I have been lying awake thinking all the time you have been reading your paper, Martin. I never had less inclination to sleep. I know that he was there looking in at me, with a smile upon his pale face. But he has gone. Thank God, he has gone! Only I can't help wondering how he came there, without our hearing his step upon the stone stair."

"Who was it, Isola?"

He knew what the answer would be. He

thought her mind was wandering, and he knew there was only one image which could so agitate her.

" Lord Lostwithiel."

"A delusion, Isa. Lord Lostwithiel is far away from Rome. Come, dear love, let me read to you again, and let us have our good Tabitha in to cheer you with a cup of tea, and to brighten up the room a little. We have been growing low-spirited under the influence of the gloomy weather."

He went out of the room on pretence of summoning Tabitha, and having sent her to watch beside his wife, he ran quickly downstairs to find out if the street door were open or closed. The door was shut and bolted. The servants on the ground floor had not opened the door to any one after five o'clock. There was no possibility of any stranger having entered the house since that hour.

The end came that night, with an appalling suddenness. Isola had refused to be carried back to her bedroom at the usual time. She seemed to have a horror of going back to that room, as if the shadows lurking there were full of fear. Even Father Rodwell's presence, which generally had a soothing effect upon her nerves and spirits, failed to comfort her to-night. She refused to lie in her usual position, and insisted upon sitting up, supported by pillows, facing the doorway at which her fancy had evoked Lostwithiel's image. She would not allow the door to be shut, and there was the same strained look in her too brilliant eyes all the evening.

Father Rodwell read aloud to her, going on with a history of St. Cecilia, in which she had been warmly interested; but to-night he could see that her thoughts were not with the book. He went on all the same, hoping that the sound of his voice might lull her to sleep. The wind had gone down as the night advanced, and the stars were shining in the strip of sky above the Pincian Gardens. Colonel Disney was pacing up and down the loggia, smoking his pipe in the cool darkness—full of saddest apprehensions.

Her mind had been wandering, surely, when she had that fancy about Lostwithiel, he told himself. It was something more than a dream. And then he remembered those long nights of delirium after her boy was born—and above all, that one night, when she had fancied herself at sea in a storm, when she had tried to fling herself overboard. He knew now what scene she had re-acted in that delirium, what the vision was which her wandering mind had conjured out of the empty darkness.

The priest left them before eleven o'clock, and Martin Disney sat with his wife till long after midnight—Tabitha waiting quietly in the next room—before he could persuade her to go to bed. Isola was more wakeful than usual—though her slumbers had been much broken of late—and there was a restlessness about her which impressed her husband as a sign of evil.

"Is the storm over?" she asked, by-and-by, with her face turned towards the loggia and the starlight above the garden.

"Yes, dearest, all is calm now."

"And the boy?" she said, suddenly looking up at the ceiling above which the child slept with his nurse. "He is asleep, of course."

"I hope so. I went upstairs at nine o'clock, while Father Rodwell was reading to you, and gave him my good-night kiss. He was fast asleep."

"I wonder whether he will ever think of me when he is a man?" she said musingly.

"Can you doubt that? You will be his most sacred memory."

"Ah," she replied, "he will never know——"

The sentence remained unfinished.

"Will you carry me to my bed, Martin? The room begins to grow dark," she whispered faintly. "I can hardly see your face."

He lifted the wasted form in his arms, and carried her with tenderest care into the next room, and to the pure white bed which had been made ready for her, the long net curtains parted, the coverlet turned down. He laid her there, as he had done many a night during that slow and monotonous journey towards the grave; but her gentle acknowledgment of his carefulness was wanting to-night. Her head sank upon the pillow, her pale lips parted with a fluttering sigh, and all was still.

This was how the end came—suddenly, painlessly. She died like an infant sinking to sleep.

Colonel Disney laid his wife in the place she had loved, the cemetery under the shadow of the old Roman wall, in a verdant corner near Shelley's grave.

Burial follows death with dreadful swiftness in that southern land, and the earth closed over Isola before noon of the day after her death.

Martin Disney waited to see the new-made grave covered with summer's loveliest blossoms before he left the cemetery and went back to the house to which he had taken his fading wife in the radiant Italian springtime. He paced the desolate rooms, and wandered in and out between the drawing-room and the sunny bed-room, with its snowy curtained bed, and looked at this object and that with tear-dimmed eyes and an aching heart.

She was gone. That page of his life was closed for ever. And now he had but one purpose and one desire—to settle his account with the scoundrel who had destroyed her. He had waited till she was at rest: and now the long agony of waiting was over. Nothing could touch *her* more; and he was free to bring her seducer to book.

He had telegraphed in the morning to Captain Hulbert at Venice, but there had been no reply so far; and he could only suppose that Allegra and her husband had left the city upon one of those excursions which his sister had described to him as diversifying their quiet life in their palace on the grand canal. He had not been at home long, and his tired eyes were still dazed and blinded by the flood of sunlight which the servants had let in upon the rooms after the funeral, when a telegram was brought to him.

It was from Brindisi.

"The *Eurydice* went down with all hands last night, off Smyrna. My brother was on board. I am on my way to Greece. If you can be spared go to Allegra.—Hulbert."

Martin Disney knew later that it was between eight and nine o'clock that the *Eurydice* struck upon a rock, and every soul on board her perished.

The boy and his nurse went back to Trelasco under Tabitha's escort, and they were followed to Cornwall soon afterwards by the new Lord Lostwithiel and his wife, who established themselves at the Mount, to the great satisfaction of the neighbourhood, where it was felt that the local nobleman had again become a permanent institution. Allegra and her husband took Martin Disney's son under their protection in the absence of his father, who carried a heavy heart back to the jungle and the tent, trying to find distraction and forgetfulness in the pursuit of big game, and who did not revisit the Angler's Nest till two years after his wife's death, when he returned to live a tranquil life among the books in the library which he had built for himself, and to watch the growth of his son, whose every look and tone recalled the image of his dead wife. Sometimes, on drowsy summer afternoons, smoking his pipe under the tulip tree, while the Fowey river rippled by in the sunshine, it seemed to him as if Isola's pensive loveliness, and the years that he had lived with her, and the tears that he had shed for her, and the infinite pity which had blotted out all sense of his deep wrong, were only the transient phases of a long sad dream— the dream of a love that never was returned.

"And yet, and yet," he said to himself, after

lengthened meditation, with unseeing eyes fixed upon the movement of the tide, " I think she loved me. I think her heart was mine from the hour her tears welcomed me back to this house, until her last sigh. God help all young wives whom their husbands leave alone in their youth and beauty to stand or fall in the hour of temptation ! "

Idly exploring the contents of the secretaire in the drawing-room one day, Martin Disney found the telegraphic message which his wife had written—and left unsent—before the Hunt Ball.

END OF VOL. II.

LONDON : PRINTED BY WILLIAM CLOWES AND SONS, LIMITED,
STAMFORD STREET AND CHARING CROSS.

www.ingramcontent.com/pod-product-compliance
Lightning Source LLC
Chambersburg PA
CBHW020939120726
47905CB00008B/2591